"I DON'T NEED YOU TO TELL ME WHETHER I SHOULD FLY!" ROSS SHOUTED.

Leia's lips parted in disbelief and her eyes grew wide. "You've never even considered it, have you?"

"What?"

"The possibility that something could happen to you up there."

He stood and glared at her. "Flying is my life, and if you want me, you're just going to have to accept that."

"You're just letting that fighter jock ego rule your reason. I thought you were more of a man than that."

"Lady, I make no excuses for who I am." Ross's hazel gaze bored into her.

"Then maybe I'm not the woman you want," Leia said softly, and stood to leave.

CANDLELIGHT ECSTASY CLASSIC ROMANCES

CANDLELIGHT ECSTASY ROMANCES®

QUANTITY SALES

Most Dell Books are available at special quantity discounts when purchased in bulk by corporations, organizations, and special-interest groups. Custom imprinting or excerpting can also be done to fit special needs. For details write: Dell Publishing Co., Inc., 1 Dag Hammarskjold Plaza, New York, NY 10017, Attn.: Special Sales Dept., or phone: (212) 605-3319.

INDIVIDUAL SALES

Are there any Dell Books you want but cannot find in your local stores? If so, you can order them directly from us. You can get any Dell book in print. Simply include the book's title, author, and ISBN number, if you have it, along with a check or money order (no cash can be accepted) for the full retail price plus 75¢ per copy to cover shipping and handling. Mail to: Dell Readers Service, Dept. FM, 6 Regent Street, Livingston, N.J. 07039.

FLIGHT OF DESIRE

Suzannah Davis

A CANDLELIGHT ECSTASY ROMANCE®

Published by
Dell Publishing Co., Inc.
1 Dag Hammarskjold Plaza
New York, New York 10017

Copyright © 1987 by Suzannah Davis

All rights reserved. No part of this book may be reproduced or transmitted in any form or by any means, electronic or mechanical, including photocopying, recording or by any information storage and retrieval system, without the written permission of the Publisher, except where permitted by law.

Dell ® TM 681510, Dell Publishing Co., Inc.

Candlelight Ecstasy Romance®, 1,203,540, is a registered trademark of Dell Publishing Co., Inc., New York, New York.

ISBN: 0-440-12642-8

Printed in the United States of America

August 1987

10 9 8 7 6 5 4 3 2 1

WFH

*For my sister, Dr. Julie Nelson,
whose genuine interest and insight helped
make this book possible.*

*Special thanks to Gil Hitchcock, good friend
and neighbor, for acting as technical adviser
and sharing his experiences as a Navy pilot.*

To Our Readers:

We have been delighted with your enthusiastic response to Candlelight Ecstasy Romances®, and we thank you for the interest you have shown in this exciting series.

In the upcoming months we will continue to present the distinctive sensuous love stories you have come to expect only from Ecstasy. We look forward to bringing you many more books from your favorite authors and also the very finest work from new authors of contemporary romantic fiction.

As always, we are striving to present the unique, absorbing love stories that you enjoy most—books that are more than ordinary romance. Your suggestions and comments are always welcome. Please write to us at the address below.

Sincerely,

The Editors
Candlelight Romances
1 Dag Hammarskjold Plaza
New York, New York 10017

FLIGHT OF
DESIRE

CHAPTER ONE

Leia McKenzie carefully adjusted the lace gown on a bride doll, then stole another look at the tall man uncomfortably perusing the display of baby dolls. They were accustomed to browsers in The Gingerbread House. Most customers were summer tourists who came to enjoy the white sand beaches in the Pensacola area. After a few days in the blistering Florida sunshine, these visitors gladly discovered the other Pensacola attractions, including the historical district around Seville Square. Quaint shops filled the tree-lined square. Renovated wood frame cottages painted soft pastel colors offered merchandise of all descriptions. Between Labor Day and the start of the holiday season, however, fewer customers came to admire The Gingerbread House's unique selection of children's clothes and collectors' dolls. That made the lone male patron on this quiet Monday all the more intriguing.

Leia set the doll on the shelf behind the cash register and shot another glance at the man, the corners of her lips twitching into a smile. A distinct twinkle shone in her blue-green eyes as she watched him stretch out a large brown hand to touch the pink satin ribbons of a doll's bonnet, only to draw away hastily before he made contact. He shoved his hands into the pockets of his tailored slacks, and his feet shifted uneasily on the plank floor. Leia had never seen any-one so obviously out of place.

His broad shoulders were encased in a crisp plaid shirt suitable for a mild September afternoon. He reminded Leia of a lumberjack. The wind had whipped his short dark hair into disorder, lifting it in little waves like the surface of Pensacola Bay, which could be seen out of the shop's long front windows. He ran his hand through his hair in a gesture of perplexity. Leia hid her smile as she moved to his side, and decided to take pity on him.

"Can I help you, sir?" she asked pleasantly.

"Yes, ma'am, I hope so," he returned in a deep drawl, relief evident in his hazel eyes. Leia found herself fascinated by the little gold flecks radiating from the center of his irises. It occurred to her that he was a very handsome man.

He stood near six feet tall, all rangy muscle that made her feel delicate and petite in comparison. He was deeply tanned, not so surprising to anyone living in sunny Pensa-cola, yet he seemed all burnished and bronzed, his skin golden and his nutmeg brown hair highlighted with gilt. His nose was straight and a bit long and was balanced by a strong jaw. There were laugh wrinkles at the corners of his eyes, and Leia knew that when he smiled it would be with a wide, engaging grin. He was older than she had first thought, perhaps in his mid-thirties, yet his lean body was evidence of a vigorous life-style. It had been a long time since Leia had felt such a tug of immediate attraction. She pulled her thoughts together with an effort.

"Are you interested in one of our baby dolls?" she asked.

"Well, ah—you see . . . ." He stammered to a halt. Leia was puzzled.

"Perhaps you could tell me how old the child is who will receive it," she suggested. "Is it for a special occasion? Your daughter's birthday, perhaps?"

"My daughter? No, I'm not married," he said, chuckling. He grinned then, revealing strong white teeth. His expression was appreciative as he admired the slim strawberry blonde before him. "It's for a friend's birthday. She'll be six," he explained.

"Oh. Well, in that case, we have several very nice choices," Leia began, turning to the shelves. She picked up a pink-cheeked baby doll. "Something like this?"

"No, you don't understand. Ah . . ." Again he stopped, at a loss for words. This was obviously a new experience for him.

"Did you have something specific in mind?" she asked.

"Well, ma'am, it's like this," he explained. "Bridget's mom is expecting a baby and Bridget insists it will be a little brother."

"Oh, I see! You need a boy doll!" Leia was pleased to have at last plumbed the depths of the mystery. "Here's one," she said, passing him a short-haired boy doll clad in overalls. "And we have several others." She paused, watching him hold the doll awkwardly in his large hands. Her eyes widened as she watched the rosy color rush to his face, up his neck, and even to the tips of his ears. Her mouth dropped open in astonishment. The man was actually blushing!

"Is anything wrong?" she asked gently. Something inside Leia melted, and her heart swelled with affection. What a marvel—a man who could blush!

"Ah, ma'am, Bridget said it had to be just like a real little boy, with, er—all the right parts," he said, swallowing hard. He glanced away and his color deepened. At last, understanding dawned in Leia's mind and she mentally kicked herself.

"You mean 'anatomically correct,' I believe," she murmured. She smothered a smile. "We have the very thing."

She dropped gracefully to one knee and rummaged through the cabinet beneath the shelves, oblivious to the fact that her movements had shifted the hem of her silky dress, exposing a shapely bit of thigh to his approving gaze. She removed a box, set it on the shelf, then displayed a dimpled doll dressed in blue. "Will this do?" she asked. "He has a complete layette and even wears diapers. I can undress him if you'd care to see—"

"No, that's all right," the man interjected hastily, backing away slightly as she offered him the doll. "I'll take your word for it. Could you wrap it up?"

"Certainly," she replied, leading him toward the cash register. "Actually we sell quite a few of these," she remarked, reaching for her receipt pad. She looked up and found such an expression of relief on his face that she laughed softly. Then he grinned, and her own smile widened as their laughter mingled in the quiet shop.

Ross Walker studied the pretty woman's deft movements as she wrapped the doll box in colorful birthday paper, then added a large bow. Now Bridget would get her "pretend brother" from her favorite "uncle." Bridget's desire for a real baby brother was beginning to border on an obsession. Her mother, Pamela, seemed to think a doll would appease the girl, because there were certainly no guarantees that the child due in three months' time would be a boy! And as long as Webb Anderson remained on carrier duty in the Mediterranean, Ross would do his best to ensure that his best friend's family had whatever they needed—even a blasted doll! At any rate, Ross was grateful he could cross this particular chore off his list.

He lounged comfortably against the wooden counter and admired the woman in profile. The plastic name tag she wore pinned to her dress said "Conner." Funny name for a woman, Ross thought, but somehow it seemed to fit her.

Gentle waves of reddish gold curls fell softly about her face, and her small pert nose was sprinkled lightly with freckles. Her rounded chin had a stubborn cast to it, but her mouth, now pursed enticingly as she secured the bow to the package, looked sweet and somehow a bit sensual. She reached up for a tag, stretching the fabric of her dress across her small but perfectly shaped breasts and accentuating the tiny span of her waist. Ross felt a sudden catch in his breathing, then looked away, studying her hands, which were slim and well kept.

"Here you are," Leia said, placing the package before him. Ross reached into his back pocket for his wallet and laid some bills on the counter.

"You've been mighty helpful, ma'am," he said. "I wish there was some way I could thank you." He turned on his world-famous grin. It started slow, then increased in voltage and never failed to attract interested feminine glances.

"You're not from around here, are you?" she asked, punching in the numbers on the cash register and then handing him the change.

"I'm originally from Tennessee," he replied, chuckling. "I've never lost the twang. My name's Ross Walker, ma'am."

"How do you do?" she replied, accepting the hand he extended across the counter. "I'm Leia McKenzie."

"Then why does your name tag say Conner?" he asked. Her hand was soft and delicate within his large paw. She laughed softly.

"It's actually Leia Conner McKenzie; Leia because I was born in Hawaii, and Conner is my mother's maiden name. I use Conner because it seems more businesslike, but my friends call me Leia."

15

"Well, they're both pretty," he said. His eyes traveled across her upturned face, admiring the silky clear skin and the faint almond shape of her blue-green eyes. Leia blushed slightly, then withdrew her hand.

"Thank you," she murmured. She busied herself by tearing off his receipt and placing it and the box in a large paper bag.

Ross inwardly smiled. He was under no illusions about his attraction to women. He had lived with it and exercised its power for too long to underestimate it. Yet there was a simple friendliness and a natural attractiveness about Leia that intrigued him. He made a sudden decision.

"Would you have dinner with me tonight?" he asked. Leia's eyes widened in astonishment. "To thank you for your help," he explained, a boyish grin creasing his face.

"Oh, I'm sorry, I can't," Leia said. "I have to work tonight." There was real regret in the husky timbre of her voice.

"Here?" he asked in surprise.

"Oh, no," she said, shaking her curls. She leaned across the counter and tapped a large notice taped to the front of the cabinet. "I teach a prepared-childbirth class at Dr. Burton's office two blocks over."

He looked at her skeptically. "You're a doctor, too?"

Leia dimpled. "No. I've worked as a nurse-midwife, but I gave it all up for this." She gestured lightly at the cluttered little shop. "I keep my hand in with the classes."

"I always thought Mother Nature took care of things by herself."

Leia laughed, shaking her head at his apparent ignorance. "It doesn't hurt to lend her a hand, and a prepared mother-to-be is a less frightened one. Easier on her and the baby."

"Hmm. Bridget's mom might be interested in that."

Leia reached under the counter and passed him a printed

16

flyer. "This has all the information about our classes, as well as my number. I'll be glad to answer any questions."

"Thanks. I'll see that she gets it." He folded the paper and stuck it in his back pocket. His eyes twinkled. "And I have a question: when do you get through tonight?"

Leia pinkened prettily. "We usually don't finish up until around ten, so it would be much too late."

Just then the little bell on the front door tinkled and a tiny, frowsy-haired woman burst into the shop.

"Oh, Leia! I'm sorry I'm so late!" Elizabeth Dexter cried, her leather shoulder bag swinging madly from its strap as she bustled toward the rear counter. Wispy strands of gray hair fell forward into her face from her lopsided topknot, and she irritably brushed them away. She shrugged rapidly out of her tweedy jacket, throwing it and her purse toward a countertop and missing completely. "You just run along," Elizabeth instructed briskly. "I'll help the customer. Now, what can we do for you, young man?"

"We're all through, Elizabeth," Leia said calmly. She smiled affectionately at the older woman, then handed Ross his package. "Thank you very much. Come again."

"Thank you!" he replied. He sketched a brief salute. "I'll sure do that!"

Leia watched him stride confidently through the front door, the package tucked securely under his arm. She was sorry that she had not been able to accept his invitation, impulsive as it was. She wasn't worried that she knew next to nothing about him. His concern over the right choice to please a little girl despite his own embarrassment had told her all she needed to know. And was he gorgeous! She sighed. She had not really been interested in anyone seriously since Mitch died. But sometimes the loneliness was almost overwhelming.

17

"What did you say, Elizabeth?" Leia asked, coming back to the present.

"I said, why do all the hunks in this world have to be married?" Elizabeth said. She stooped to pick up her coat, then slung it onto the seat of a nearby chair.

"Who?" Leia asked, blinking.

"Don't give me who," Elizabeth groused. Her iron gray eyebrows arched expressively on her wrinkled forehead. She nodded toward the front door. "That who!"

"Oh, him! He's not married." Leia laughed.

"He's not! Well, did you get his name? How about his telephone number? You know you've got to be aggressive if you expect to get a man these days!"

"Oh, Elizabeth! I'm not looking for a man!" Leia giggled.

"Well, you should be! It's just not right, a pretty thing like you sitting around all alone. And you're not getting any younger, you know! What are you now? Twenty-seven?"

"Twenty-eight," Leia answered mildly. She was used to her godmother's tirades by now. Their friendship was one of long-standing affection and innate understanding. Leia had come to visit Elizabeth in Pensacola each summer while she was growing up, from wherever in the world her Air Force colonel father was stationed. And now that they were business partners in The Gingerbread House, their relationship had grown even stronger.

When Elizabeth Dexter had approached Leia with the chance to invest in a struggling business, Leia had not hesitated. She knew that underneath the older woman's sometimes scatterbrained exterior was an astute businessperson. Leia had also realized that a wise investment at this point in her life could give her the stability that she had always craved. Not that she didn't enjoy her career as a nurse-practitioner and midwife, but she knew that she did not want to be forever at the mercy of shift work.

"And I'm not alone," Leia continued. "I have you, don't I?" She dropped a quick kiss on Elizabeth's lined cheek.

"Humph. And what good does a crotchety old woman do you when you go home to an empty house?" Elizabeth demanded. "Don't look at me like that, either! I've been a widow for twenty years; I know what it's like! It's been seven years since Mitch was killed, and even longer since we lost Stephen. Your brother wouldn't want you to mourn them like this!"

"I'm not mourning, Elizabeth," Leia replied quietly. "It's just that Mitch and I had something special. Even though we weren't able to get married before he died, I don't think I could ever find that kind of relationship again."

"Nonsense!" Elizabeth snorted. "You've got to give yourself a chance! Take that young man who just left. He was interested; I could tell by the look in his eye. Why, with just a bit of encouragement, you could find yourself in the middle of a sizzling love affair!"

"Elizabeth!" Leia gasped.

"It'd do you a lot of good," the older woman muttered.

"Well, I'm not given to casual affairs, as you know," Leia replied, laughing softly at Elizabeth's disgruntled countenance. "But I'll give it some thought," she promised.

"You do that," Elizabeth said. She pulled a pair of half-spectacles from her purse and plopped them down on the end of her blunt nose. "You'd better run along if you're to get a break before your class starts," she advised. "And that's another thing—you're working too hard! Working full-time here, and your classes, and even moonlighting sometimes at the hospital! It's too much. You know what they say about all work and no play!"

"I like to stay busy." Leia shrugged. "And it pays the bills."

"Your father would help out with the mortgage if you'd

just ask him," Elizabeth said with a sniff. "A colonel's pay isn't too shabby, and he can't have very many expenses, not now that your mother has remarried."

"That's not the point." Leia sighed. "I made the decision to invest on my own and I'll pay my own way. It's just a matter of time before the shop begins to show more of a profit. Then I'll ease off."

"If it doesn't kill you first!" Elizabeth commented.

Leia laughed. "Hard work never hurt anybody."

"And you had to go and move into a new house now, too!"

"I was tired of apartments," Leia replied. "It's a nice quiet neighborhood, and it really isn't costing me much more than I was paying for that apartment." She gestured toward a stack of boxes lined up against the rear wall. "By the way, the delivery man came. I only got a chance to go through a portion of the shipment, but it appears most of the Christmas merchandise has come on time for once."

"Good. I'll go through it," Elizabeth said, settling her glasses more firmly on the tip of her nose and waving Leia toward the door. Leia smiled as Elizabeth tore into the first box, her satisfied clucks and murmured "Darlings!" reflecting her pleasure at the array of holiday dresses and tiny velvet suits. Although Elizabeth's lectures had become more frequent lately, they never lasted long, and Leia knew they were motivated by love. Leia paused at the front door.

"Did I mention that one of the mothers in class does hand smocking?" she asked. "She'll let us have some of her English smocked bonnets on consignment."

"What? Oh, that's a good idea, dear," Elizabeth replied absently, checking off another item on her inventory list. "It would be a nice addition to the line we carry now."

"I'll talk with her about it again," Leia promised, then let herself out of the shop.

It did not take Leia long to get home. She pulled her small sedan into the shell drive of the white frame house. It might look a bit shabby to others, but to Leia the house and tiny yard with its massive old azalea bushes represented something she had never been able to have before——a permanent home.

She paused to pick up the newspaper from the front porch. The streets were tree-lined in this older area of Pensacola, the houses of an earlier generation now mostly inhabited by young families. In the brief time she had been in her house, Leia had met several women whose husbands were stationed at the naval air station that was just a twenty-minute drive to the southwest. The neighborhood was quiet at this time of the day, but soon there would be hordes of schoolchildren playing on the cracked sidewalks and on the vacant lots at the end of the street.

Leia unlocked the door, then dropped her bag on the kitchen counter as she scanned the headlines. She kicked off her shoes and padded barefoot across the polished wooden floors through her sparsely furnished living room to the bedroom. The house held an eclectic mixture of Leia's possessions. Some things, like the carved wooden screen from the Philippines, she had acquired in her years as an Air Force brat, while others, like the golden oak washstand, she had found in antique shops. In the bedroom was a massive burled dresser and Shaker-style four-poster bed she had ordered from a catalog. Several colorful quilts lay atop the bed.

Leia only noticed these things in passing as she headed for the bath. A good long soak was just what she needed to relax before her class. She always did her best thinking up to her chin in hot water and bubbles. She turned on the taps and wondered if she might be thinking too much about a certain pair of hazel eyes.

Ross stood under a streetlight in front of Dr. Leonard Burton's office just off Seville Square and wondered what the hell he was doing. He could have been visiting Pamela and Bridget, or down at the Officers' Club knocking back a few beers with the guys, but instead he was standing on the curb trying to decide whether to go in looking for a woman. Just like an infatuated schoolboy, he thought in mild disgust.

It wasn't as though Leia McKenzie was the most beautiful thing he had ever seen, either. Plenty of gorgeous women had moved through his life, but somehow he couldn't seem to get those blue-green eyes out of his mind. Lately, as always near the end of a tour, an intense restlessness consumed him. However, if he was asked what he was searching for he could not have said. Except that something about Leia—her calmness, her soft beauty, perhaps even a vague feeling that she was searching, too—drew him back to find out whether the illusion was true. That and the fact that if he didn't seek her out before he flew out tomorrow at noon, he'd have to wait almost a week before he had another chance. For a man as decisive as Ross Walker, that in itself was the clincher.

The front door of the office opened and he straightened, his eyes scanning the group coming out. Couples, a happy group, talking and laughing among themselves, all the women in advanced stages of pregnancy. Good, at least he was at the right place! A slim figure in slacks appeared at the door, her arms laden. Ross's eyes lit up and he strode forward.

"Need any help?"

"Ross!"

The pleasure on her face could not have been faked, and Ross felt a creeping exhilaration. "We never did get to finish our conversation," he said. "How'd you like to try it over a late drink?"

"I'd love to," Leia replied warmly. She juggled notebooks, purse, and sweater.

"Hard night?" he asked lightly, leaning closer. The mysterious depths of her aquamarine eyes drew him to her like a magnet. Leia made a little moue with her lips and shook her head.

"Not too bad—now." She laughed, her eyes sparkling.

His ego swelled, flattered in spite of himself at her obvious eagerness. She was like a breath of sweet, clean air, nothing coy about her. It made a change from the usual vacuous, airbrained women who followed him and his teammates around.

They stood on the sidewalk. The night air was cool, the breeze carrying a hint of salt from the Gulf.

"Where would you like to go?" Ross asked, helping her slip into her sweater. He was near enough to inhale Leia's fragrance, an intriguing mixture of clean soap scent, delicate floral perfume, and woman.

He tugged the sweater snugly into place at her neck, then deliberately raised her chin, stroking the tender underside of her jaw with his thumb. He could feel the delicate flutter of her pulse beneath her skin. Ross could not resist the tempting, petal-soft mouth lifted to his, slightly parted with surprise, but making no attempt to avoid him as he lightly brushed her lips with his own. Her mouth was as sweet and adorable as he had imagined. Although he was tempted to deepen the kiss, he drew away. She smiled shyly, and there was a new awareness between them.

"Where do you want to go?" he repeated. He let his hands fall away.

"Uh, I don't know. You decide," Leia suggested a bit breathlessly.

She deftly tucked an escaping curl back into the soft, elegant knot at her nape, fiddling momentarily with the clasp that held it. Ross waited to see if she would loosen her hair and was disappointed when she did not. Unexpectedly his spirits lifted. Perhaps he would get the chance to do it himself later on.

"Well, there's Cowboys, or Rosie O'Grady's, or we could even drive out to Kevin's on the beach," he suggested easily. He scratched his chin thoughtfully and kicked the curb with the toe of his shoe. "Or there's always my place."

"Really, Ross!" Leia laughed and he joined in, glad she had not taken offense at his teasing remark. He touched the small of her back and guided her down the sidewalk toward his car, liking the feel of her beneath his fingertips, while they continued to wrangle good-naturedly over their choices. Suddenly Leia drew up short.

"Is this your car?" she asked in a strange voice. Ross glanced at her, then at his low-slung, fire-engine-red Corvette.

"Yeah." He tugged his ear. He was accustomed to his women friends being awed by his car, but not terrified of it. Then he noticed that she was staring wide-eyed at the blue bumper sticker that identified him as an officer.

"You—you're in the service?" Leia asked.

Ross clicked his heels and bowed deeply. "Lieutenant Commander Ross E. Walker, United States Navy, at your service, ma'am," he said with a grin.

"What do you do in the Navy, Commander?" she asked, turning abruptly to stare at him, her voice a thin thread of sound.

"I fly jets, ma'am," Ross replied proudly.

"Oh, God!" The whisper was wrung from her, and her face blanched as she placed trembling fingers to her lips. Alarmed, Ross stepped forward to cup her elbow, but she jerked away, her blue-green eyes wide with horror. Ross wondered if he had suddenly sprouted horns and a tail.

She took another step back. "I—I'm sorry—" she jerked out in a strangled tone. "I can't—I'm sorry!" she finished helplessly, then turned and ran back up the sidewalk as if the devil himself really did pursue her.

"Leia! Leia, wait!" Ross shouted, but already she had disappeared back inside the building. He stood poised to go after her, baffled, and yet with the first stirrings of anger the impulse to follow her died. He had no idea what had precipitated her flight, but no woman had ever turned down Ross Walker!

"Women!" he muttered, flinging himself behind the wheel. "Who needs 'em!"

CHAPTER TWO

"I just don't know what happened, Elizabeth," Leia said miserably. "I feel so rotten—and ashamed."

Elizabeth Dexter poured coffee into a large glazed pottery mug and passed it to her goddaughter. As she replaced the pot on the single burner of the hot plate that made up their "kitchen" at The Gingerbread House, she noted the dark circles under Leia's eyes.

"I can see that the experience upset you," Elizabeth murmured.

Leia's laugh was rueful. "I'm a wreck," she admitted.

She sipped the hot, aromatic brew and sighed. A sleepless night had been the result of her flight from Ross Walker's presence. At dawn she had not been able to stay in bed any longer. Needing her reassuring presence, she chose instead to join Elizabeth early at the shop. Leia set the mug down on the scarred table with a thud.

"Worse than that," she continued, her voice laden with self-disgust. "I feel an absolute fool. A perfectly nice man, and at best I only hurt his feelings and insulted him. He had to wonder what kind of loony he had gotten mixed up with!"

"Well, why don't you call him up and apologize?" Elizabeth suggested.

"Oh, no, I couldn't!" Leia gasped.

"Where's your pride? You owe him an explanation, at least," Elizabeth said reasonably.

Leia shook her head. "It would be too awful."

"Well, suit yourself." Elizabeth shrugged, but her expression showed her disapproval.

"I don't know how to get in touch with him," Leia said, knowing the excuse was a weak one.

"Call the naval air station. I'm sure they'll know," the older woman replied.

"I suppose so," Leia agreed despondently. She knew she was being childish, and that fact on top of her strange behavior the night before was wreaking havoc upon her peace of mind. "I guess I'll feel guilty until I do." The corner of her mouth tilted. "How does it feel to be right all the time?" she teased.

"Get on with you!" Elizabeth scolded. Leia laughed lightly, then moved through the small doorway that connected the back workroom to the front of the store.

Once at the counter, her hand hesitated over the telephone. What could she possibly say to Ross Walker that would make any sense? She closed her tired eyes for a moment as she gathered her resolve. She had to make an attempt or Elizabeth would never let the matter rest.

Surprisingly, and a bit to Leia's dismay, it was a simple matter of talking to Base Information to acquire Lieutenant Commander Walker's office number. The brisk voice that answered the phone identified himself as Yeoman Reynolds but informed Leia that the commander was out, was not expected back, and could he take a message?

"Ah—this is Conner McKenzie," Leia began. "Just tell him—no, never mind. It doesn't matter. Thank you," she stuttered. Shaking, she hung up the phone.

"No luck?" Elizabeth asked. Leia shook her head, ashamed at the relief she felt. The truth was, she was too embarrassed to face Ross Walker again and too afraid that his very presence would summon forth the mindless fear and panic that had so surprised her the previous evening. She had been secure too long, and had become a bit too complacent about her ability to handle that fear again. Somehow the shock of learning that the man—that special, perhaps even wonderful man—was a pilot. . . . Involuntarily she shuddered, pushing back all the black memories.

"I might try again sometime," she lied shakily. She wiped her damp palms down the sides of her pants legs, then straightened the collar of her tailored jacket. "I think I'll tag those play clothes."

Elizabeth gave her a searching look, then shrugged. "I wouldn't mind the help. I've got to write up that ad, too."

The women worked in silence for the next hour, rapidly attaching sales tags to an assortment of summer clearance merchandise. They made a good team. They kept their working schedules flexible but tried to have most of the tedious inventory work done before they actually opened the doors at ten.

Leia was on the floor, up to her elbows in a large box of assorted knit shirts, when there was an imperious rap at the still-locked front door.

"Seems we have an early customer," Leia remarked, smiling. But her smile froze on her lips and her laughter died when she raised her head and saw the tall figure silhouetted on the front porch.

"You'd better go let him in, honey," Elizabeth said softly as Ross Walker knocked again. Woodenly Leia rose and made her reluctant feet carry her across the store. Her fingers were cold as she twisted the bolt and drew it back, forcing herself to open the door.

They stared at each other for a long, awkward moment. Ross's expression was hidden behind dark, gold-rimmed sunglasses. Very deliberately he unhooked the wire stems from behind his ears and took off the glasses.

"Morning, ma'am. Were you looking for me?"

His drawled words were innocuous enough, but the glitter of gold in his hazel eyes was chilling. Leia's mouth worked but nothing came out, and she clutched the edge of the door with nerveless fingers.

Ross stepped forward, forcing Leia to retreat from his massive presence, opening the door wider as he entered the store. A little gasp escaped her lips as she took in his appearance.

Gone were the casual slacks and shirt. Instead he wore a royal blue one-piece flight suit that fit his lean, muscular body like a second skin, emphasizing the breadth of his shoulders and the trimness of his narrow waist. The ascot beneath the zippered collar at his neck was brilliant yellow-gold, as were the bands running vertically down the left side of his chest. Centered on the bands were the neatly embroidered letters of his name, his rank, and the number 3. And on his right breast was the insignia of the Navy's most elite squadron—the air demonstration team known as the Blue Angels. Inwardly Leia groaned. Not only was the man a pilot, he was a hotshot fighter pilot, an aerial daredevil!

Ross removed the peaked khaki cap he wore and waited, staring down at Leia, his handsome face set in granite lines.

"I called to—to apologize," Leia said faintly. Out of the corner of her eye she saw Elizabeth disappear into the back of the store. Traitor, she thought a bit hysterically.

"Oh?" Ross pressed the door from Leia's grasp and allowed it to slam shut hollowly behind them. Leia swallowed. She could tell that he was not going to make it easy for her.

"I'm really very sorry, and I hope you'll understand that I—I had a reason for what I did." She faltered, a rosy tide of embarrassment flooding her cheeks.

"Well?" The word was a demand for further explanation. Leia fell back another step as Ross moved closer.

"Ah, it's personal," Leia murmured. She chewed her lips, and her blue-green eyes were harried.

"Come on, Conner," Ross rumbled gruffly. "You've got to do better than that!" When Leia hesitated, he glanced at his wristwatch in irritation. "Look, sweetheart, my butt's going to be in a sling if I'm not back at the base in half an hour. I'll take some flak as it is. I've got to fly out of here for Seattle at noon. You owe me!"

Leia studied the thin line of his compressed lower lip and decided he was right. Her shoulders slumped.

"I know," she whispered. And suddenly two huge tears welled up in her eyes. Ross jerked back as if shot.

"Christ! Don't do that," he said, aghast. Leia hastily wiped the moisture from her eyelids with her fingertips.

"I know, I'm sorry," she said huskily. She fumbled for a tissue in her jacket pocket, sniffed loudly, then lifted her chin with touching fortitude. "You see, I lost someone I loved deeply, and he was a pilot, too. I didn't know you . . ." She trailed off, then began again. "It—it was just the shock, you see. I am dreadfully sorry, Ross. Please forgive me," she finished in a rush.

Ross cleared his throat and moved his feet uneasily. Her frankness had disconcerted him.

"Ah, it was your husband?" he asked softly.

Leia shook her head. "My fiancé. In Air Force flight training." She paused, then continued, relentlessly assessing the depths of her loss as if by doing so she might somehow cauterize the gaping wounds. "And also my brother. He was shot down in Asia."

"Christ!" Ross's exclamation was low and fervent. Tentatively his hand touched her arm. "What can I say?" he murmured.

30

Leia shook her head, strangely comforted by the warmth of his hand on her skin. "It was a long time ago." Her slight smile was crooked. "I still tend to surprise myself sometimes. I'm sorry my problem had to involve you, though."

"I'll let you make it up to me," Ross replied. His expression had softened almost to tenderness. "We still haven't had that drink together." Leia swallowed and licked her suddenly dry lips.

"I don't think it would be a good idea under the circumstances," she said.

Ross's hand tightened on her arm. "Why?" he demanded arrogantly, his eyes narrowing.

"Surely you can see—"

"No, I don't see anything," he interrupted sharply. He again glanced at his watch. "Look, I don't have time to stand here arguing. I'll be back at the end of the week. I'll give you a call then." He released her arm and slapped the peaked cap back into place on his dark hair.

"It would be better if you didn't bother," Leia protested faintly. Ross paused at the door, giving her a searching look that traveled from her head to her toes.

"Believe me, ladybird," he said, a wicked gleam in his eyes, "it won't be any bother!"

Leia felt the hot color rise to her face. "But, Ross!" she protested again.

Ross was already through the door. "I'll see you, Leia!" he promised, vaulting down the wooden porch steps. He jumped into his red car, gave a quick wave, and then roared out of the quiet square with a squeal of tires as he gunned the powerful engine.

Leia stood on the porch watching him disappear with a feeling of dismay and foreboding. Just like Mitch, she thought, chewing her lip. Mitch had loved fast cars, too. He got high on speed and a sense of his own immortality as he

31

handled a rocketing piece of machinery. It was something Leia had never understood in spite of how much she loved him. And now Ross. She closed her eyes for a brief moment and prayed that he wouldn't keep his promise.

Ross braked slightly as he slid past the saluting guard at the guard post entrance to the naval air station, then automatically shifted the powerful car into a higher gear. He raced down the broad tree-lined boulevards that bisected the base, made a turn, and headed for the area known as Sherman Field, the home of the Blue Angels. He pulled into his parking place beside the huge hulking hangar that housed the squadron offices, grabbed his kit, and set off at a jog toward the entrance.

On the stretch of landing field behind the hangar, "Fat Albert," the squadron's Lockheed C-130 Hercules transport, was being readied for takeoff. Twelve and a half tons of squadron personnel and equipment would precede the team to this week's show site in the fat-bodied aircraft with its distinctive blue, gold, and white markings, sported by no other aircraft in the Navy.

Farther down the flight line stood the six sleek McDonnell Douglas F/A-18 Hornets, their navy blue and gold paint gleaming brightly in the morning sun. A versatile supersonic aircraft used by the Navy since 1978, the F/A-18 was a relative newcomer to the Blue Angels. Ross loved flying the powerful jet, which could almost literally change from fighter to attack aircraft at the flick of a switch. Pilots who flew the F/A-18s liked to say that under combat conditions they could fight their way in, drop a payload, and fight their way out again. Ross increased his pace, heading for the group of other team members standing on the pavement near the hangar. They were due shortly in the squadron briefing room to begin the routine of preflight preparations.

"Cuttin' it kinda close this morning, ain't you, Ross?" Commander Chuck Lohman, the team's commanding officer and flight leader, said. Ross grinned at the lanky blond man, known to the team as "the Boss." If one didn't know better, he would think Lohman had just come off the farm and probably still had hayseed in his hair. But the Oklahoman's laid-back personality was only the facade of a man whose leadership ability had been proved time and again and who could count almost four thousand hours of flight time and better than five hundred carrier landings.

"Sorry, Boss!" Ross said, saluting smartly. "Had a few last-minute details to attend to."

"Don't believe a word of that bull," Lieutenant Sanderson "Sandy" Howell, the team's opposing solo pilot, remarked. "It's got to be woman trouble." He slapped his cap on his russet hair, and his freckled face creased in a grin.

"Who, him?" Captain Jason "Skip" Stillworth hooted. His blond California-boy good looks belied the fact that he was a skilled tactical pilot. An officer of the Marine Corps, Skip flew right wing to Ross's left wing in the famous diamond formation that was the Blue Angels' trademark.

"Take my word for it," slot pilot Lieutenant Commander Bill "Alcatraz" Crane assured them in his Texas drawl. "Reynolds told me she sounded real sweet, too!" The group dissolved into laughter at his high-pitched mimicry.

"Now, don't be too hard on old 'Hickory,' here," solo pilot Lieutenant Commander Marc "Miami" Garret said, defending Ross. He caught Ross in a friendly headlock, and the two dark-haired men scuffled playfully for a moment before breaking apart. "He just might be nursing a broken heart!"

Ross grinned, taking no offense at the good-natured ribbing. He and his fellow Blues were linked by bonds as strong as brotherhood. Countless hours of training together, eating, sleeping and dreaming jets together, had forged ties of affection and respect that would last the rest of their lives.

"Well, if it's as serious as that, then you'd better marry the girl, son," the Boss said.

"Hey, give me a break!" Ross protested. The group snickered collectively as they envisioned the squadron Romeo hitched at long last.

"You're gettin' too old for that stuff," Lohman advised in a serious tone, but his pale blue eyes twinkled. "Always said a married man was more stable. Me and Crane are 'bout the only ones with a chance of surviving the season, leastways unless we run into one of you crazy bachelors up there!"

His remark elicited groans and protests from the unmarried members of the team. For an instant Leia McKenzie's face flashed in front of Ross's eyes as he had last seen her—eyes tear-washed, expression vulnerable, beautiful, and desirable. In that moment he tried molding her into the pattern of fantasy wife—would she fit, or were the edges of her experience too ragged? He shook off the notion. Better wait until he was back in Pensacola to figure that one out.

"All right, let's go," Lohman ordered, jerking a thumb toward the hangar. As they moved toward their preflight briefing, the group of men continued to rag each other in good-natured camaraderie, but Ross was strangely quiet and preoccupied.

The Saturday crowd had thinned somewhat when the pretty, dark-haired woman entered The Gingerbread House. Leia was busy ringing up a sale, but she couldn't help smiling at the pregnant mother dragging her very reluctant gamine-faced pixie toward a rack of party dresses. The little girl was five or six, with large dark eyes and a short mop of black hair. She clutched a grimy doll under one arm, and there was something vaguely familiar about her.

Leia handed her customer her change and went over to the woman. "Can I help you?"

"Well, maybe." She smiled, then caught the little girl's shirt just before she disappeared underneath the rack of clothes. "Biddie, behave! We've got to get you a nice dress for church."

"I don't wanna dress. I want jeans!" piped the youngster indignantly.

"Looks like trouble," Leia said and laughed.

The woman sighed. "All the time," she admitted ruefully. "Are you Leia?" she asked suddenly. "You must be. Ross said you were pretty."

"Ross?" Leia was startled.

"I'm sorry. I tend to babble on anyway, but it seems to get worse when I'm expecting." She smiled and rested her hand on her protruding stomach. "I'm Pamela Anderson, and this is Bridget. Ross got her birthday present here the other day."

"Oh, the doll!" Leia nodded in understanding.

"She hasn't put him down for a minute, which accounts for him looking like he's been dragged through a knothole backward!" Pamela laughed. "But I think a doll should be played with, don't you?"

"Absolutely!" Leia returned her smile, caught up in Pamela's bubbly personality.

"His name is Bubba!" Biddie volunteered.

Leia dropped down on one knee and smiled at the child, dutifully admiring the proffered doll. There was still something familiar about the little girl. Suddenly she knew what it was. "Say, Biddie, don't you have a red bike?"

"I sure do! And I don't even need my training wheels like stupid ole Jeremy!"

Leia glanced up at Pamela. "I've seen Biddie riding

35

around my neighborhood. I moved into a house on Garden Street about a month ago."

"How nice! We're just a block over on Perdido. How do you like it?"

Leia stood. "I love the neighborhood. Everyone's so friendly. And it sure beats apartment living."

"I know what you mean."

"Mama, Mama!" Biddie interrupted. "Do you think they got any clothes for Bubba here?"

"As a matter of fact, we do," Leia replied. She pointed toward a display next to the doll counter. "Go look right over there."

"Okay!" Biddie skipped off.

"I still can't believe that Ross actually had the nerve to buy that doll himself," Pamela said, shaking her long dark hair. "It doesn't at all fit in with that cool image he likes to project."

"He was *very* uncomfortable," Leia admitted. They laughed together.

"But he came through, as always," Pamela said. "I don't know what we'd do without him. My husband's on carrier duty in the Mediterranean, and it's nice to know there's someone I can call on if I need to."

Leia made a suitable murmur of agreement. Ross Walker was one subject she didn't want to discuss. Just the thought of him could make her burn with embarrassment and then go cold with apprehension. "Could I show you some dresses, Mrs. Anderson?"

"Please, call me Pamela. *Mrs. Anderson* makes me feel so old," she said with a laugh. "We do need a dress, and I wanted to find out more about these childbirth classes. I didn't get to take them when Bridget was born."

"There are sessions going on all the time. I'll be giving

several more before you're ready to deliver," Leia told her. "Will your husband be home by then?"

"Webb should be getting leave just about that time. I thought I might attend the classes and send him the materials to study beforehand."

"That would work, but it really would be easier on you if you had a substitute coach to attend with you. Many of my mothers do it that way. Anyone can do it. A good friend, either a man or a woman. I have one woman whose mother-in-law is her coach."

"Hmm. I'll have to give it some thought." Pamela grinned suddenly. "Maybe I could talk Ross into doing it."

"Well . . ." Leia looked skeptical.

Pamela placed her index finger on the side of her cheek and narrowed her eyes thoughtfully. "Bad idea, huh?" Her mouth curved into a puckish grin. "Still, it wouldn't hurt to put him on the spot for a change. He's always teasing me."

"Then it would serve him right." Leia laughed, pulling a sailor dress out of the rack. "Now how about something like this for Biddie?"

By the time she left The Gingerbread House, Pamela was signed up for Lamaze classes to begin in several weeks, Biddie had, under protest, agreed to two new dresses and been mollified with a new outfit for "Bubba," and Leia felt that she had made two new friends.

"Lady, I have a bone to pick with you."

Leia stared at the telephone receiver and wondered if this was how an obscene phone call began. "I—I think you have the wrong number," she said, her voice faltering.

"Hold it! Leia, this is Ross Walker."

"Oh. Hello," she said awkwardly. She reached over and flicked off the Sunday-night drone of the television and

37

threw down the pencil she'd been using to work the cross-word puzzle in the Sunday paper.

"What's this I hear about a conspiracy between you and Pamela to make me some kind of coach?" he demanded.

Despite herself, Leia chuckled. "I swear it was all Pamela's idea."

"I'll bet. I'll get you for this one," he promised. "So, how've you been?"

"Fine."

"Are you ready to settle up?"

"Settle up?" Her tone was puzzled.

"You owe me one, remember? How about if I pick you up at about seven tomorrow evening?"

"No, I don't think that's a good idea."

"Busy, huh? What about Tuesday?"

"I have classes on Tuesday, but that's not what I meant and you know it!"

"Look, Leia, I thought we had been through this before."

Leia stifled a sigh. "Ross, I'm sure you're a very nice man, but—"

"I'm better than nice," he interrupted. "I'm stupendous, or at least I was until I met up with you. Now my confidence is battered. I may never be able to function again."

"Stop it. I feel guilty enough as it is."

"Good. Hold that thought. I may shrivel up completely unless you agree to go out with me. Think of all the deprived females in the world. Do you really want the suffering of all womankind on your conscience?"

Leia tried to hold back a laugh. "Now, Ross . . ."

"Come on, ladybird. You owe me. I'm harmless. A nice dinner, a little conversation? You know I won't give up. I'm not that kind of man. And let me warn you, when I'm thwarted I can be a real pest."

"Harmless, huh?"

"Relatively."

Leia sighed and rubbed her forehead. She knew he was telling the truth. She'd never met anyone so determined, or with such complete confidence in his own appeal and abilities. And after all, what harm would it do? She knew she represented a challenge because of the abrupt way she'd left him the other time. Maybe if she agreed, he would move on to the next pretty face. She knew she wouldn't allow herself any emotional involvement, no matter how attractive she found him.

"Pick me up at seven."

"Good move, Leia." His voice was husky.

"Just be warned, I eat like a horse, so bring your wallet," she said on a shaky laugh.

"A little ladybird like you?" he said scoffingly.

"Don't say I didn't warn you." She gave him her address and said good-bye. It was hard not to wonder if she'd lost her mind.

"I can't eat another bite!" Leia said. She set her fork beside her half-finished slice of cheesecake. She looked at Ross across the candlelit table. His gray suit and tie and white shirt set off his dark good looks to breath-catching perfection. He wore the formal garb with the same ease and aplomb as he did his flight suit.

"You disappoint me. And here I'd made a major bank withdrawal just to cover your dinner," Ross said easily.

"So I can't eat as much as you, you big ox!" she said with a laugh. "I admit it. But it was wonderful. I've never eaten at Coppersmiths before. Thank you."

"My pleasure."

The waiter appeared with the bill and Ross dealt with it while casting covert glances at Leia. She was wearing some green silky thing that made her eyes look emerald, and her hair fell in soft curls about her face. Her cheeks were becomingly pink, and her features looked soft and lovely in the dim light.

Good, he thought, she's lost that nervous look. When he'd picked her up she'd been pale and tense. He'd set out to be charming, demanding nothing, and now she was beginning to relax with him. Not that the atmosphere hurt.

Coppersmiths was the elegant central restaurant at the core of Seville Quarter, a renovated warehouse that was a popular entertainment complex in downtown Pensacola. Connecting sections included Rosie O'Grady's, where one could hear Dixieland jazz, Phineous Phogg's Discotheque for pop music, and for country and western there was the New Orleans—style courtyard called End O' the Alley Bar.

The waiter departed and Ross stood, offering Leia his hand. "How would you like to see what's cooking in the rest of this joint?" he asked.

"I'd like that."

He guided her out of the restaurant, his hand on the small of her back. She was so feminine and petite, it made him feel protective as they worked their way through the brick-paved alleys separating the sections. He moved closer to shield her from the jostling crowd. He could smell her sweet perfume wafting up and fought a sudden urge to bury his nose in her curls.

Back off, he warned himself. Keep it light and easy. He didn't want to scare her, not when she was on the point of admitting he wasn't really an ogre. And suddenly he realized that it was very important to him that he be allowed to get to know her better.

They went into Rosie O'Grady's and listened to a set of Dixieland music with a boisterous crowd, joining in on all the choruses. They sang and clapped and laughed. Then they went outside to the courtyard to catch their breath and talk. While they listened to Tennessee pickin' music, he told her about his boyhood in the foothills of the Smoky Mountains. She described what it was like to grow up in Germany and Guam. The more she opened up, the more he wanted to learn. And the more he wanted to hold her.

"Why don't we see what's going on in the disco?" he asked finally.

Leia readily agreed, and Ross drew a sigh of relief. What more perfect excuse to put his arms around her than on a dance floor? His spirits lifted even more when they pushed through the heavy double doors and found that it was Forties Night. The sounds of Glenn Miller and the Andrews Sisters coming from the disk jockey's booth meant that he could actually touch her!

He led her down the two steps and onto the narrow, sunken dance floor.

"Good lord," she said a few minutes later. "How is it that a man your size is so light on his feet?"

"Natural rhythm and coordination." He grinned down into her upturned face. "Only a couple of my many talents."

"Modesty being one of the main ones," Leia teased.

"Well, you know what they say. When you got it . . ."

"I know, flaunt it!" They laughed together. It was so easy to laugh with him, she thought.

When the music slowed to "Sentimental Journey," Ross pulled her closer and his steps became smaller. Leia's heart raced. She could feel the heat radiating from him and smell the sharp citrusy scent of his aftershave. It was really too bad that there was that one flaw about him she couldn't live with. Yes, if he weren't a pilot, she might really be drawn to him. It was hard to resist his magnetism. She sighed slightly and matched her steps to his. She might as well enjoy the warm feeling of being close to him, knowing that it would have to end all too soon.

Ross felt her subtle acquiescence and smiled into her hair. He wasn't after an easy conquest, but he was rather proud of his technique with this skittish filly. Now, if he could just get her alone somewhere . . .

Just then he felt a hearty clap on his back. "Hey, Hickory! What'cha doing, man?"

Ross groaned inwardly. Any other time he would have been glad to run into his teammates, but not tonight! He responded with as much grace as he could manage. "Hey, you jokers! Leia, this is Sandy Howell and Marc Garret, Blues solo pilots."

Leia nodded to the two clean-cut men clad in Navy whites. Each had a beaming, lovely girl on his arm.

"This is Rita," Sandy said. "And this is Charlotte."

"Hello, you pretty thing," Garret crooned to Leia. "You can call me Miami." Leia was slightly taken aback, then smiled back in response to Miami's infectious grin.

"Cool your jets, Miami," Ross rumbled. "This one's spoken for."

"Sure, Hickory, sure. Say, why don't you join us? We were just going next door to Lili Marlene's for a drink."

Ross cocked an inquiring eyebrow in Leia's direction.

She hesitated, then shrugged. "Sure, why not?"

They left the disco and went into the small, quieter lounge, where a single guitarist played softly from the corner. In the process of selecting a table, getting seated, and ordering, Leia sneaked an inquisitive glance at Ross.

"Hickory?"

"Call sign," he muttered. "You know. Tennessee. Andrew Jackson. Old Hickory."

"Makes sense." Leia's eyes sparkled. "I suppose."

The conversation was lively, filled with gay banter and aviation jargon. She noticed that none of the men had anything stronger to drink than ginger ale, an indication that they would be flying on the morrow. Leia let the talk flow around her, and she was filled with a bittersweet nostalgia. There was a poignant familiarity to her presence here. It had been a long time, but she had once been accustomed to being around men who loved flying.

"God, it's been years since I was there," Miami was saying. "Let's go give it a look-see. It's only across the square from here."

The group was agreeing to his suggestion, but Leia had lost the train of the conversation.

"Are you game?" Ross asked.

"Where?"

"A place called Trader John's. We used to hang out there when we were in training here. It's a bit rough."

"All right, but after that I really should be getting home. Some of us have to work for a living, you know." Her smile was impish.

"You're a peach, Leia," Ross said, squeezing her shoulders.

They left Seville Quarter and walked across the street-lamp-illuminated square and down the block. The other couples talked animatedly, but Leia and Ross walked behind quietly. They came upon the rough board-sided facade of Trader John's Bar, and Leia followed the others through the heavy door.

She glanced with little interest at the bare concrete floors and the long expanse of bar down one side of the cavernous interior. At a pool table lighted by a single dangling bulb, groups of young Navy men, immediately identifiable by their short haircuts, played eight ball. It was at least cleaner than most dives, she supposed.

Leia looked around, puzzled by a sudden growing sense of unease. Suddenly she blanched and her heart refused to pump the blood through her vessels. Her lungs would not draw air into her lungs. Her lips parted on a tiny gasp of terror and she realized that she had walked right into her own personal hell.

CHAPTER THREE

There was no relief anywhere! Everywhere she turned, they stared out at her! Handsome pilots in full regalia, framed and hung for all time. Some were perched in the cockpits of their killer machines, some stood on the flight line. From the walls, the ceilings, they reached out for her, the heroes of other years. Their banners dangling, the engraved invitations dusty from time, the model airplanes hovering, the smiling, autographed photos were arranged in permanent disarray to amaze and amuse. It was a macabre museum, a Blue Angel shrine.

Crushing claustrophobia reached out and squeezed her heart. Blindly she turned to flee, but she didn't know the way out.

"Leia? What's wrong?" Ross's voice came from far away.

She couldn't answer him. An empty Blue Angel flight suit hung nearby, the breeze of their passage making it stir with a mockery of life. A soft cry of revulsion escaped her.

"Leia?" His large hands pressed her shoulders.

"Get me out of here, please." She felt as if she were choking, her teeth chattering.

"Sure." His voice expressed his mystification and concern. With a few words to the others, he steered her out the door and into the cool night air. Several paces down the sidewalk he drew her headlong, panicky flight up short.

"What is it?" he demanded, taking in her chalky countenance. She shuddered and shook her head wordlessly. Frowning, he wrapped his arms around her trembling form in the only comfort he knew.

Leia buried her face in the fabric of his jacket. Already the fresh air had calmed her. She took a shaky breath. "God, that was awful."

"What? What happened back there?"

"All that stuff. I felt like—like I was in some sort of tomb. A grisly shrine. Didn't you feel it?"

"What, all that aviation memorabilia? The fellow who owns that place is a Blue Angel fan from way back. For God's sake, it's just a bunch of keepsakes, just a collection of harmless junk!"

Leia sensed his exasperation, his confusion, and knew she couldn't explain her unexpected gut reaction. How could she tell him that it was as though she had opened a door to a part of her own brain that made her want to scream and scream and scream? She pulled away from him, biting her lip at his perplexed expression.

"I knew this wasn't a good idea," she mumbled. He started to protest, but she cut him off. "Please. Please, just take me home."

Ross's jaw hardened. "Right," he said. He grabbed her and quick-marched her toward the parking lot.

Worn out by the stressful end to a lovely evening, they barely spoke as Ross negotiated the darkened streets. He pulled up in front of her house and came around to open her door. The subdued chirp of crickets and the gentle swish of the Gulf breeze through the trees was all that could be heard. Streetlights made spots of brightness along the dark street, but Leia's house looked abandoned and lonely, since no welcoming light burned within.

46

They walked silently to her porch and stood awkwardly while she searched for her key and stuck it in the door.

"Does it make you nervous to enter an empty house?" Ross asked softly. "I'll be glad to look around for you if you want."

Leia smiled at his innate courtesy. "I'm all right, but thanks. And thank you for the evening, too. It was lovely."

Ross jammed his hands into his pockets and jingled his change and keys restlessly. "Look, ladybird, I'm sorry you got upset back there, but you have to admit we were doing pretty well before you got the jitters."

Leia sighed. Her tone was rueful. "Seems I'm always getting upset around you. I'm the one who should apologize, Ross. I wish I could convince you that I'm really a fairly stable person. I'm not normally so spooky."

"Hey, I'm already convinced." His smile was a band of white in the darkness as he leaned against a post. "But I'll give you all the chances you want. Would you like to do something tomorrow?"

Leia's smile faded. "N-no, Ross. I'm sorry, but my first instincts were right. It would be better if we didn't see each other again. It's not fair to you."

"Let me be the judge of that, Leia." He stroked her arm, raising goose bumps. "If you wanted to be fair, why'd you agreed to go out tonight?"

"I just wanted to make up for the way I acted before."

"Is that right?" he asked, his voice silky.

She sensed a sudden charge of annoyance beneath his smooth tones and was alarmed. The pressure of his arm increased, drawing her closer.

"You haven't begun to make up for that mistake," he murmured.

She wanted to demand to know what he meant, but her words were swallowed by his heated lips slanting across her open mouth. A jolt of electricity surged along Leia's nerve endings, numbing her under the warm onslaught of sensuality. She heard herself whimper deep in her throat. Then there was nothing to do but give in to the magic of Ross's persuasive embrace.

Without thinking, she relaxed her body against his hard length and her hands slipped up the solid bulk of his chest to clasp around his neck. Her nostrils were filled with the male smell of him, musky and warm and with a hint of citrus. The stubble of his beard rasped pleasurably against her tender skin as he tasted and probed and sent her spinning mindlessly into a whirlwind of desire.

Sensing her response, Ross deepened the kiss, losing himself in her sweetness, pressing her soft form to his hardness and filling his palms with the essence of her womanly curves. She followed where he led, but soon it was a dance with no leader, their passions unleashed and whirling like dervishes as they stood locked in a timeless world of sensation.

Leia's breath stopped in her throat, and she tore her lips away, gasping. "No more," she pleaded, clinging to him.

She was trembling, her hands clenching the fabric of his shirt and her face buried in his chest. His lips traced the tender juncture of her hairline, and she could feel his warm breath, as ragged as her own, on her forehead. The violence of their reaction to each other both elated and frightened Leia. She listened to the pounding of his heart as it slowly subsided beneath her ear.

"Leia, you are full of surprises," he murmured at last. Leia's head jerked up and she searched Ross's face for some understanding of what had just occurred. She pulled back as much as he would allow.

"I'm tired. I—I need to go in," she stammered. Suddenly the enormity of her response filled her with humiliation. She could not meet his eyes. Ross shoved his fingers into the golden red strands of her hair, his fingertips trailing erotically against her scalp. He gently turned her face up to his.

"What's wrong?" he breathed softly against her lips. "Something just happened here . . ."

"Nothing happened!" Leia said quickly. "Nothing at all!" She pulled away from him.

Ross's expression was perplexed and showing the first signs of temper. "Nothing except that you went up like a flame when I touched you!" he growled. "And don't blame it on fatigue! I didn't take advantage of you, and you know it! Now tell me what's frightened you."

"Nothing," Leia whispered miserably.

He rubbed the back of his neck in a gesture of bewilderment, then sighed deeply. "Look, we've got to talk this out, but not tonight. I'll call you tomorrow."

"No!" Leia's response was curt.

"No? What the hell's the matter with you?" he demanded, exasperation in his voice.

"Just because you kissed me, nothing has changed. Don't you understand?" Leia cried, her tone panicky. "I will not get involved with a pilot! I've told you why!"

"Leia, it's too late for that," he replied with a strange, humorless laugh. "You're already involved."

He caught the nape of her neck in one large paw and kissed her again, hard. Leia was powerless to fight the compelling sensations his mobile mouth evoked. When he finally pulled away, she was bemused, her senses muddled.

Ross reached behind her, opened the door, and gently pushed her into the dim confines of her house. His soft words taunted her.

"Now go to bed and sleep on that."

Leia stepped onto her tiny front porch and sniffed the Sunday-evening air with pleasure. October was still warm in

49

Pensacola, but the days had begun to shorten and there was a hint of fall in the salty breeze. She sat down on the concrete step and tightened the laces of her jogging shoes.

She adjusted her ponytail and began to go through a series of warm-up exercises, her legs extended in a hamstring stretch beneath her peach-color jogging suit. Jogging was another reason Leia loved her new neighborhood. Not an addicted runner, she ran for the chance to be outdoors whenever possible and to relieve stress.

Not that what she suffered from since her disastrous date with Ross Walker the previous week could be called stress. It was more like free-floating anxiety. She ought to be glad that he hadn't called, yet she doubted that a man of his determination had given up so easily. She was constantly waiting for the ax to fall, mentally rehearsing all the good reasons she shouldn't see him again. That her arguments were more to convince herself than him was something she didn't want to examine too closely, especially in the light of her volatile reaction to his kisses. She had been on edge, her defenses up, waiting for the moment to firmly but kindly refuse to see him again. It was definitely anticlimactic to find that her trouble had been for nothing. She wondered if his silence was some sort of psychological warfare.

Shrugging at the thought, she decided that she had worried long enough about Ross Walker. He'd taken the hint, she told herself firmly, and resolved to put him out of her mind. She jogged off down the sidewalk, trying not to think about the unique color of his eyes.

She ran down Garden Street at a moderate but steady pace, waving to the elderly couple who lived in the house on the corner and side-stepping a game of hopscotch being played by three little girls. The car belonging to the young couple in the yellow house was missing. Had they taken a Sunday drive? The smell of barbecuing meat wafted from

50

the rear of the brick ranch house. Must be a party, Leia mused, her ponytail bobbing. As she listened to the rhythmic splat of her rubber soles against the pavement, she tried not to feel lonesome amid the homey sights and sounds.

Leia turned the corner onto Perdido Street and came upon a calamity. A red bike lay sprawled half in the gutter, and a small figure sat in the grass between the curb and sidewalk, holding her knee and snuffling.

"Biddie?" Leia pulled up short, breathing rapidly with exertion. She dropped down onto the grass beside the dark-haired urchin, her nurse's eye noticing the torn pants leg and the bloody and tattered flesh of a badly skinned knee. "Oh, dear, you've hurt yourself, haven't you? I'm Leia. Do you remember me?"

"Uh-huh." Biddie nodded, her large dark eyes filled with tears. She bit her lips, struggling valiantly not to cry.

"Let me see," Leia said gently. "I'm a nurse, you know." She examined the knee, clucking sympathetically. "I know it hurts, Biddie, but it's not as bad as it looks. Can you walk? We need to get it cleaned up. With a big bandage on it, you'll be good as new."

"I can—can walk," Biddie said with a hiccup, knuckling her tears away.

"You live on this street, don't you?" Leia asked, helping her up. "Here, I'll bring your bike."

"Right down there," the little girl replied, pointing.

"Okay," Leia said cheerfully. "Let's go."

They made a strange procession, Leia helping Biddie hobble down the sidewalk while pulling the little red bike behind, but it only took a minute to reach the small blue-sided house. Biddie led Leia toward the carport door, calling loudly for her mother. Leia leaned the bike against the house, then did a double-take and nearly groaned out loud. There in the carport beside a white station wagon was a shiny red Corvette. She didn't even have to guess whom it belonged to.

"Biddie, what happened?" Pamela Anderson's rounded figure stood in the doorway.

"I had a wreck," Biddie answered, "and Leia found me."

"Well, thank goodness for Leia!" Pamela bent awkwardly to look at the injured knee. "Oh, Biddie, what a mess! And you even tore your new pants!"

"I don't think it's too bad, Pamela." Leia began to edge away, anxious not to meet Ross again, if indeed that was his 'Vette in the carport.

"Mama, she's a nurse," Biddie piped. "Can she fix my knee? Please?"

"Oh, I don't think—" Pamela began.

"Please?" Biddie's lower lip trembled.

"How can you resist a plea like that? What do you say, ladybird?" Ross asked suddenly.

Leia jerked, startled by his appearance in the doorway behind Pamela. He was darkly handsome and neatly dressed as always, this time in a soft blue knit shirt and khaki slacks. His eyes pierced her, and a golden-flamed awareness crackled between them. Leia's breath caught, her senses enmeshed by his rugged looks and his vibrant magnetism. She tore her eyes away from him with an effort.

"I don't mind bandaging Biddie's knee at all," she told Pamela.

"Well, if you're sure, I'd appreciate it."

Minutes later Biddie sat importantly on the table in the modest kitchen and Leia bent over her, working with cotton and antiseptic. She tried to ignore Ross as he watched her every move, but she found his intense regard disconcerting. She placed a large bandage over the scrape and taped it firmly in place.

"There, all done," she said with a smile. "Biddie's been a very brave girl, Pamela."

"I'm always brave," Biddie bragged. "I din't cry when I had my 'peration and Daddy din't even know about it till he got off the boat!"

Leia cast a puzzled glance at Pamela.

"She had an appendectomy during Webb's last tour. Life with our Biddie is always interesting," Pamela said with a wry twist of her lips.

"I understand," Leia said with a laugh, helping Biddie down.

"Will you stay awhile, Leia? We were just watching a football game on TV," Pamela said. "Ross used to play in college and he was giving me the play-by-play."

"No, I can't. Thank you, but I've got a heavy day tomorrow. We've got a big sale starting in the morning. Why don't you come over? We'll be open later than usual," Leia replied.

"I just might do that. I need a few things for the new baby," Pamela said. "Are you sure you can't stay?"

Leia cast a swift glance at Ross. "I'm sure, thanks. I was jogging when I found Biddie and I'd like to finish my round before it gets too dark."

"You and Ross! I just don't understand people who run and say they're having fun," Pamela said with a smile.

"We're a different breed, all right," Ross said.

"Yes, well, ah—I don't think Biddie will have any trouble with that knee." Leia edged toward the door, keeping her eyes averted from Ross.

Ross felt his jaw clench in annoyance at Leia's obvious reluctance to be around him. Why was it so easy for this woman to get under his skin? Why did it bother him so much that he couldn't make any headway with her?

Hell, he thought in disgust, she had been up front with

him. Why couldn't he take the hint and stay out of her life? But when he looked at her, all pert and tidy in her childish ponytail and that stylish running suit, he couldn't help but remember the way she felt in his arms and the softness of her mouth on his. She was an intriguing mixture of prim lady and passionate wanton, and he longed anew to discover her secrets.

"I'll see Leia out," he said. He took Leia's elbow and felt her stiffen tensely beneath his touch.

Pamela looked curiously at him, then noted Leia's flushed cheeks. She made no comment other than to thank Leia again for her help, inviting her to stop in anytime.

Ross walked outside with Leia, guiding her through the narrow space between the cars in the carport.

"So, how have you been?" he asked.

"Fine."

Her monosyllabic answer irritated him, but he noticed that she licked her lips nervously. "Lucky you found Biddie when you did."

"I was glad to help. She seems to be more than a bit accident-prone."

"Unfortunately for Pam."

Leia looked thoughtful for a moment. "What—what did Biddie mean about her father not knowing about her operation? Why would Pamela keep something like that from her own husband?"

Ross was silent for a long moment, and Leia's cheeks flushed with embarrassment. "I'm sorry. Forget I asked. It's none of my business."

"No, wait." He laid a restraining hand on her arm, and they paused on the sidewalk in front of the house. "It's a bit hard to explain, but it's not because there's anything wrong with their marriage. It was a Navy wife's decision."

"I don't understand."

"When you're on sea duty, you make carrier landings every day." Ross's voice took on a faraway sound. "It's hard to describe a landing. You've got to hit a bouncing, heaving deck going full-throttle, so that if the tail hook misses, you can gun her up into the heavens again. If you don't, you end up in the drink. When you're making a landing you can't be thinking of anything else, or you may wind up a pile of scrap metal on the carrier deck." He returned his full concentration to Leia. "Pamela knows that, just like every other Navy wife. If she chooses not to tell Webb about Biddie's operation until he gets home, or passes her little accident today off lightly, then that's her way of protecting him, of making sure he comes home."

"I'm not sure I like the sound of that," Leia said slowly.

"Well, in this case, ignorance is bliss, as they say." He shrugged.

"If you were in that position, would you want to know?"

"Hmm. Good question, ladybird." He mulled it over a moment. "Probably not, unless there was something I could do about it. And stuck out there in the middle of the ocean, there wouldn't be a whole hell of a lot I could do—except worry—and that could be hazardous to my health. Sometimes in a partnership, one partner has to contribute more than the other, but then it evens out in the long run."

"It doesn't sound very even to me," she replied. She rolled her neck, stretching muscles she had unconsciously tensed.

Ross saw her movement and reached over to massage her shoulders and neck though her peach warm-up jacket. Leia couldn't suppress the tiny murmur of languorous pleasure his strong fingers elicited. Their eyes met and there was a moment of awkward silence.

"I—I'd better go," she faltered.

"Leia, let's try it again," he said softly, looking down into her eyes, wide and as blue-green as a tropical pool. His fingers moved persuasively against her shoulders.

"What would be the point?" she asked, a sorrowful helplessness making her voice husky. She caught his wrists, tugging gently until he released her.

Ross jammed the flat of his palms into his back pockets and frowned. He worried at the crack in the sidewalk with the toe of his shoe for a moment, then shot her a glance that held nothing of defeat in it. A half-grin cocked his mouth at a rakish angle.

"You know, if I thought you were playing hard to get, I wouldn't waste a minute here, but I think you really mean it."

"I'm trying to." Unexpectedly she felt her own smile of amusement. It was hard not to like this man with his wry humor and supreme self-confidence.

"Well, ladybird," he said in his drawl, "I can see I'm going to have to change my tactics. My ma raised me to be polite, but I'm gonna quit *asking*. I don't like the answers I've been getting lately."

"Sorry about that."

"Don't fret your pretty head about it, ma'am," Ross said, thickening his drawl into a hill-country twang. "Just remember, all we've had so far are a few skirmishes. Things will change when I go to a full-scale attack."

He caught her chin and gazed down into her astounded face. His slow grin rattled Leia more than she wanted to admit. She caught her breath, certain that he was going to kiss her right here on the sidewalk, but then he chuckled and released her.

"See you, ladybird."

He disappeared back into the Anderson house and Leia jogged away in the diminishing light, hoping that her knees would support her until she could get home.

* * *

The Monday of The Gingerbread House's big sale had been more successful and hectic than Leia or Elizabeth could have foreseen. It was gratifying to see the cash register totals at the end of the day, but Leia knew from the ache of her tired feet how hard she'd worked.

It was after dark when she got home that evening. She had just kicked off her heels and was contemplating the merits of peanut butter versus canned tuna when the doorbell rang. Grumbling under her breath, she padded to the front door. Peeking out the front window, she recognized the tall silhouette and gave a start of surprise.

She opened the door, a questioning look on her face. "Ross? What are you doing here? Is something wrong?"

"The situation is desperate!" he cried, dramatically clutching a loaded brown paper bag to his chest and raising his face to the heavens. "You see before you a man virtually on the point of collapse!" He opened one eye and sneaked a look at her.

"Collapse from what?" she asked suspiciously.

"From hunger!"

"Are you looking for a handout?" Leia asked, incredulity fighting with laughter. Ross composed his handsome features into lines of wounded dignity.

"On the contrary! Would I come empty-handed after you've put in a hard day selling tiny little garments to half the mommies in the city of Pensacola?"

"I don't know," Leia said and laughed. "Would you?" She fought desperately to hang on to her composure, but she didn't know what to make of this high-spirited version of Ross Walker.

"Absolutely not!" He dug into the bag and passed her a loaf of crusty French bread, a head of lettuce, then a pair of long-stemmed wineglasses. Reaching into the bottom of the

57

bag, he removed a lid, and immediately the savory aroma of spaghetti sauce teased Leia's nostrils. She released an involuntary sigh of pleasure.

"I knew you couldn't resist my culinary masterpiece!" he said. "Now do I get to come in, or are we going to eat it standing on your porch?"

"You cooked?" Leia squeaked, her eyes wide with surprise. Her burdens shifted precariously in her arms.

"But of course!" Ross replied loftily. "Now where's the kitchen?"

Out of self-defense Leia fell back, allowing him to enter, and she trailed behind him as he carried his offerings toward her kitchen.

"I don't know about all this," she said dubiously. She gingerly lowered her parcels to the small kitchen table, then rubbed her tired neck. "I seem to remember an old quote about Greeks bearing gifts . . ."

Ross's rich laughter rumbled deep in his chest and he grinned boyishly while unloading the contents of his bag. "There's also one about looking a gift horse in the mouth," he retorted. He finished his task, then came to stand in front of her. "Busy day?"

She nodded, and his hands came up to rest lightly on her shoulders, massaging away the tiredness.

"Hungry?"

Again she nodded.

"Then why don't you change and let me finish getting dinner ready? Okay?"

Leia stared up at Ross, mesmerized. He exuded an animal vitality and energy that was exhilarating to her benumbed senses. He was full of himself, cocky, self-assured, and very, very attractive. She was totally unable to resist him. Slowly she nodded, and his smile grew even wider.

"Don't worry about a thing," he said, hustling her out of the kitchen. "I'll find what I need."

Leia chose to ignore the flashing red warning light that was blinking off and on in her subconscious. Instead she allowed herself the luxury of a quick, refreshing shower, then donned a soft blue pullover and her favorite pair of jeans. She brushed her hair out of its tight businesslike coil, enjoying the feel of it against her shoulders. A light coat of lip gloss was her only concession to Ross's presence. She smiled as she listened to the opening of cupboard doors and the banging of pots in the kitchen.

When she came out into the living room, however, Ross was investigating the contents of her bookshelves. He rocked back and forth on his heels, his hands jammed into the back pockets of his navy slacks, his eyes narrowed as he read the titles. The cuffs of his striped dress shirt had been rolled up to reveal his tanned forearms. He turned and grinned engagingly when she appeared.

"That's better." He nodded in approval, taking in her more relaxed attire. "Pretty heavy reading material here," he commented, running a finger along the edge of a tall shelf.

"Mostly my medical books, but I've been known to read a best seller on occasion," she said with a smile. Ross came to a group of picture frames scattered among the books, and Leia stiffened. He paused with his finger touching the metal frame that held a photograph of a young man with an aviator's wings.

"And this?" he questioned softly.

"My brother, Stephen."

"I see the resemblance now." His finger moved to another picture frame, and his eyebrows lifted in a mute question. Leia swallowed and licked her lips.

"That's Mitch, just before he went off to flight school," she said quietly. Ross's finger hesitated, then moved on.

"That's my father," she supplied hastily, pointing to the next picture of a distinguished man in an Air Force colonel's uniform. "He's desk bound now due to medical problems, and he hates it. And the next one is my mother, Adele, and my stepfather, Sam Milke, on their wedding day," she finished.

"And Mrs. Dexter, too, I see," Ross added, picking up a china frame.

"We're not related. I'm her goddaughter," she explained, taking the picture and glancing at Elizabeth's lined visage affectionately. She looked at Ross curiously.

"Do you have family, Ross?" she asked.

He grinned suddenly, flashing his brilliant smile. "Hell, yes! Haven't I mentioned them? Five brothers and sisters, Ma and Pop, and hordes of nieces and nephews, all back in Cumberland, Tennessee."

"My goodness! Do you see them often?"

"I usually take some of my leave time every year for a nice long visit," he replied. "They're just simple folks, but we love each other."

"How lucky you are," Leia murmured softly.

Ross shot her a sharp glance, then bowed gallantly. "Your table awaits, ma'am," he said. "And I don't know about you, but I'm so hungry I could eat a Tennessee warthog—raw!"

Leia laughed and allowed herself to be escorted into the tiny kitchen. She stopped short at the scene that awaited her.

Ross had found her red-checked place mats and napkins and arranged the table, complete with fresh flowers and lighted candles. He seated her with a great flourish and told her to begin her green salad while he opened the wine.

"This dressing is delicious," Leia observed as he poured the hearty burgundy into their glasses.

"Walker family recipe. Play your cards right and I may share it with you someday."

Leia flushed slightly at his playful words and turned her attention to her salad. When they had finished, Ross removed their plates, then replaced them with platters of spaghetti and meatballs, liberally sprinkled with grated Parmesan cheese and accompanied by hot garlic bread. Leia's amazement knew no bounds.

"I can't believe you actually cooked this," she said at one point. "It's wonderful!"

Ross attacked his generous portion with all the gusto of a starving man. He laughed at her as he deftly twirled spaghetti into a ball on his spoon and popped it into his mouth.

"I should be insulted, but I see you've done justice to my cooking," he said, nodding at her clean plate. "Which is just as well, because I don't do desserts."

"Oh, I couldn't anyway!" she said. She pushed her plate away and rested her elbows on the table, her chin in her hands, watching him with awe as he proceeded to polish off not two but three servings!

"Amazing," she marveled in a teasing voice.

"What?" Ross's tone was lazy with contentment as he sipped the last of his wine.

"That you can eat like that and not become the size of an airplane hangar! And that you actually like your own cooking that much!" Leia laughed.

"A confirmed bachelor has to develop the fine skill of self-preservation," he retorted. "Since the Blues make so many personal appearances as part of the recruiting effort, I have to eat an awful lot of bad banquet meals and cocktail buffets. Home cooking is a luxury, even if it is my own!"

Leia, emboldened perhaps by the unaccustomed wine, let slip the question that popped into her head.

"Why haven't you ever married?" Her heart leapt into her throat at the sudden blaze of gold in the depths of his hazel eyes.

"I haven't had the time or inclination, or met the right woman—until now," he said deeply.

Leia stood abruptly, bumping into the table in her agitation and rattling the dishes. She caught her glass before it toppled, and turned away. She could feel Ross coming to his feet behind her and fled into the living room.

She jumped when he laid his hand gently on her shoulder. "Don't be afraid of me," Ross pleaded softly into her ear.

Leia closed her eyes against the barrage of conflicting emotions that flashed through her. She felt Ross's large hand give her shoulder an encouraging squeeze.

"Give us a chance, Leia," he said.

"You don't know what you're saying," she replied. She laced her hands around the bowl of the goblet and drank deeply of the rich deep wine, seeking courage in its burgundy depths.

Ross gently turned her to face him. "On the contrary, I know exactly what I'm saying."

Leia searched his face in an effort to understand just what was happening between them, but all she could think about was how attractive he looked with his dark brown hair falling across his forehead. Her fingers itched to touch his hair, to twist her fingers in the thickness of it. She swallowed.

"You don't know me well enough," she protested.

"Leia, I know all I need to know," he replied seriously. He took the glass from her and set it down. His hands again captured her shoulders, and his thumbs rubbed unconsciously along the slender column of her neck.

"I know you're intelligent, educated, ambitious, and cool

62

in an emergency, even if it was only a skinned knee. You're loving, compassionate, good with kids, and very, very beautiful," he said, his voice husky. He drew her unresisting body closer. "And I know that you don't hate me as much as you want to believe."

He lowered his mouth almost hesitantly and kissed her, his lips warm and sensual. Leia swayed against him, resting against the hard wall of his chest. As he pressed her closer, she longed to melt beneath his skin, to become part of him in a communion of intimacy.

She could no longer deny it to herself. He had touched the frozen core in her heart and melted it. It was a relief, but at the same time it was threatening. If she could feel this way, then she could be hurt again.

"There," he said, lifting his mouth from hers, a note of wry humor in his voice. "That wasn't so bad, was it? *I* wasn't so bad?"

His request for reassurance was almost touching. Leia opened her bemused blue-green eyes and trembled with the realization of how much she liked him—and how much more she could like him!

"It's not you," she murmured. How could she make him understand? "It's the life you represent."

"Tell me." He drew her down beside him on the couch and held her hands, watching her earnestly. Leia bit her lip and glanced away.

"I saw the military life destroy my parents' marriage. Not just the constant moving, but the stress of living with a man who feels himself invulnerable, a bit more than other men. Then, losing my first love and my brother, whom I adored— I refuse to accept any more misery!" His hands stilled on hers as she spoke, and now she looked directly at him, baring her soul with as much honesty as she possessed.

"If I let myself—care for you," she whispered, "I'll be

right back in the same kind of cruel situation that it has taken me so long to recover from!"

"So you keep me at arm's length even when you know in your heart there could be something very special between us?"

"Yes." She shivered. "I have to."

Ross touched her cheek, then pushed a red-gold strand of hair behind her ear. Leia trembled as his fingers trailed down her neck. His expression was earthshakingly tender, his smile so gentle it melted her bones.

"Leia, let it happen," he said, pressing her palm to his heart. "Our love can be the shining barrier that protects you from harm." Her expression was amazed, and he laughed softly. "Am I taking you too fast?"

She nodded.

"Then I'll slow down, but don't expect me to stop now that I've found you. Let me show you that it won't be impossible for us."

"But Ross . . ."

"I know it won't be easy. My schedule takes me away most of the week, but we could work on it."

"How can you be so sure?" she wondered, dazed.

"Trust me."

He gathered her close, nestling her head against his broad chest. When he was this close, she felt dizzy and had a hard time organizing her thoughts. Or was that due to the wine? She tried to remember why she should be protesting, but it felt so good lying in his arms that she did not want to worry about that now. Her eyes closed sleepily and she knew a deep contentment, marred only when she suddenly developed a case of hiccups. She felt Ross's chest move with laughter under her cheek.

"You're very lovely," Ross murmured, tipping her chin

upward so that he could look into her glazed eyes. He lightly kissed the tip of her nose. "You are also a tiny bit drunk!"

"Am I?" Leia asked, blinking.

He laughed at her owlish expression. "Yup. Now, release me, woman, and I'll gather up my paraphernalia and leave you in peace." Leia sat up reluctantly, and he grinned. "Never let it be said that I took advantage of a tipsy lady!"

Leia smiled, a little Mona Lisa smile that promised untold delights, and Ross groaned. He kissed her briefly, then pulled away, and Leia wasn't sure if she was pleased with his restraint or not.

In short order Leia stood at the front door wishing him good night.

"I'll call you when we get back."

"Back from where?" she asked muzzily.

"Arizona, this week. Take care, ladybird."

When he was gone, Leia was uncertain whether she was sorry or glad. His presence brought forth turbulent emotions that were better left untapped. She needed time to rebuild her shattered defenses. She should be glad that he would be halfway across the country for the rest of the week. Why, then, did the thought leave her feeling so alone and bereft?

CHAPTER FOUR

"Where have you been?" the deep voice demanded through the phone receiver.

Momentarily startled, Leia hesitated. "Ross?" she ventured.

"I've called a dozen times. Do you know what time it is?"

He sounded so much like an irate father that Leia couldn't suppress a laugh. "I had to work late. I just got home." She kicked off her shoes and curled up on the sofa.

"I was worried," he admitted. The noise of a crowd drifted across the conversation.

"Were you?" A warm feeling surrounded Leia's heart. It had been a long time since anyone but Elizabeth had expressed concern for her welfare.

"Yeah. So, how've you been?"

"Fine. Are you still in Phoenix?"

"Yup. One more show tomorrow. Can you hear the noise? I've been turning on the old charm for the PR people tonight."

Leia laughed. "Hardship duty, huh?"

"You can't imagine." His voice lowered. "God, I've missed you, Leia! I can't keep you out of my mind."

A thrill shot through Leia, but common sense warned her not to admit that he had pervaded her thoughts over the past few days. She cast about for a safe subject. "I—I saw

66

Biddie and Pamela in the shop today. Biddie's knee is almost healed."

"That's good. Has the weather held there?"

"It's gotten a lot warmer again." She was faintly puzzled by the question. Had he called for a weather report?

"Great! Maybe we can make one last trip to the beach when I get back. Look, I've got to go. The Boss is breathing down my neck."

Leia heard a comment in the background denying the accusation and laughed again. "Be careful tomorrow, okay?"

"Sure, ladybird. Always."

"And, Ross?" She hesitated, then decided to tell him the truth. "I—I'm glad you called."

She could almost see his grin, that little smile that started slow and broadened into something devastating.

His voice was husky. "Me, too. See you soon."

Leia slid the phone from her ear, then held it under her chin while she chewed on her bottom lip. Why did she let him charm her so? What was it about this man that could slip under her defenses with such absolute ease? She was courting disaster even to think about him. She gave herself a mental shake. Time to be firm with him—and herself! There would be no trip to the beach, either! He was a nice man, but just because he made her heart go pitty-pat didn't mean she had to behave like a schoolgirl! She knew where she was going in life and she couldn't afford to get sidetracked by the likes of some good-looking flyboy!

Besides, she thought with a sigh, he was so gorgeous he probably had to beat the women off with a stick! What did he want with a long-in-the-tooth ex-nurse whose idea of a hot time was soaking her aching feet? No, he was merely amusing himself with her, Leia decided, despite all his sweet words and promises. He would soon tire of the game. She hung up the receiver with a decided click. It was up to her to protect her heart, so that when he did, she would have no regrets.

Ross shifted his packages and peeked through the door at The Gingerbread House a few days after their telephone conversation. Good, he thought, not much early afternoon activity. He allowed his gaze to caress Leia's pretty profile as she worked on the doll display. She arranged the lace christening gown on a china baby doll, her head bent in concentration. He sucked in a breath between his teeth. She was so damn soft and lovely. It made a man's hands just itch to hold her! But he had to tread lightly or she'd run like a spooked rabbit for sure.

His mouth went suddenly dry at the thought. He couldn't let that happen. There was something special about this lady, something precious and fragile, yet strong and resilient all at the same time. He ached in a region of his heart that hadn't been touched since he'd had a crush on Mary Jane Monahan when they were both eight. Leia was special, all right, with a bewitching kind of innocence that kept him tied in knots, and for a man used to plenty of willing women, that in itself was an astonishing admission.

He wasn't going to let her reservations stop him from exploring the enticing possibilities she offered, albeit unwittingly. He was a man of determination. What he wanted he went after. He squared his shoulders under his blue flight suit. What he wanted was Leia Conner McKenzie.

"Hello, ladybird."

"Ross! What are you doing here?"

Her smile was a delight that stunned his senses. He found himself grinning back at her. "Just a little PR work." He presented the single red rose with a flourish.

"Oh, how sweet!" She sniffed the flower's delicate fragrance, then eyed him suspiciously. "PR work?"

He held up a large brown envelope and grinned. "All in the line of duty. I've got a batch of autographed pictures to hand out in the children's ward at Baptist Hospital."

"Oh, I see."

"And if on my way I just happen to also run into a certain gorgeous lady, then that's just one of the perks of the job." And a little PR in that department can't hurt, either, he thought to himself wryly.

Leia laughed, blushing slightly. She walked to the back counter and placed the rose in a bud vase. Ross followed her as she began to busily straighten boxes of girls' knee socks that weren't in any need of attention in an effort to hide her nervousness. She had lectured herself firmly to resist this man's charm, but he exuded charisma, radiating strength and vitality that tugged at her senses in waves of attraction. She felt as helpless as a butterfly in a net.

"I'm sure the children will enjoy your visit," she murmured, glancing at him from under her lashes.

"I like this part of my job," he replied, lounging easily beside her and watching her deft movements. "The kids remind me of the nieces and nephews back home."

She looked at him curiously. "So it isn't entirely the flying? You really don't mind the public part of being a Blue Angel?"

"Not a bit!" He spread his hands dramatically. "I'm here to represent the best in naval aviation. And what's not to like?"

Leia couldn't repress her chuckle at his cocky swagger. "Pretty sure of yourself, aren't you?"

His expression sobered, and he leaned closer. His voice was low, intimate. "Only in some things, Leia."

"Ross . . ." she began uncomfortably.

"Why don't we go out tonight so we can make sure of a few things together?"

"I can't. I'm sorry." She averted her eyes, backing off subtly.

Ross's mouth tightened, but he was too determined to let her off so easily. "Why not?"

"I've got to teach a prepared-childbirth class that's beginning tonight," she explained. "In fact, Pamela is signed up for it."

Ross had the impression that she was grateful for the excuse, valid as it might be, but he hid his annoyance behind a lazy smile. "So you mean the only way I'll be able to see you is if I agree to be Pam's Lamaze coach?"

"Looks that way." Leia's chin lifted in challenge. "Are you up to it?"

Ross tugged at his ear and shifted sheepishly. "Well, now, that's a pretty hard bargain you're driving, ma'am. I mean, I'm fond of Pam and all, but . . ."

"I thought you'd promised your friend Webb to help out," she reminded him, arching her eyebrows.

"Well, yes, but damn! I'm not even married!" he sputtered. A rush of color flooded his skin under his tan.

Leia laughed softly, but not unkindly. She patted his hand. "I'm sorry, Ross. I shouldn't tease you. You should only do it if you feel comfortable with it. But it's not as though you'll have to be there for the actual birth, is it? Isn't Webb supposed to be back by then?"

He rubbed the back of his neck. "Yeah, well, I suppose."

"Whatever you decide, I'm sure Pamela will understand."

"Yeah, sure." He shifted the fat envelope of pictures and grinned crookedly. "I guess I'd better go. See you."

In his car on his way to the hospital, Ross wondered how he had been so neatly outmaneuvered by such a little soft slip of a woman. But he had never been one to shun a challenge and he wasn't about to start now. Even if it meant embarrassing the hell out of himself at a damn Lamaze class! The thought made him swallow hard.

At seven o'clock that evening Leia welcomed her new students to their first prepared-childbirth class. She had about ten couples signed up, typified by very nervous and uncertain husbands and their very pregnant wives. The meeting room in Dr. Burton's office filled rapidly, and Leia could not conceal her surprise, or her pleasure, when Pamela Anderson showed up with Ross in tow. Pamela filled out the registration forms, chatting to Leia animatedly about Biddie. Ross, looking too large and masculine for the small carpeted room, held Pamela's obligatory two pillows and shifted awkwardly in his shoes.

"I don't know how you did it," Pamela said in her bubbly manner, her dark curling hair falling from a simple ribbon band. "But I'm grateful, Leia. I'm so relieved Ross agreed to be my temporary coach."

"I'm sure Ross made the decision himself and not because of anything I said," Leia replied with a smile of approval for the man in question. She indicated the open area where the class would be held. "Why don't you find a place on the floor and we'll get started?"

Pamela agreed and waddled off. Ross followed, but as he passed Leia, he leaned down to whisper in her ear. "Don't kid yourself, ladybird. This isn't *just* for Pam. You owe me—again."

Leia tried to keep her mind off his unsettling words while she conducted the class, but she was supremely conscious of Ross the entire time. She lectured on anesthesia and postnatal care, and introduced the first set of relaxation exercises. During the discussion of focal points, she knew his attention was focused right on her, though she didn't dare meet his eyes. She ran through the series of breathing techniques used during labor, giving the mothers-to-be the assignment of practicing the first method until next week's meeting. She dismissed the class with a heartfelt sigh of relief. She hadn't imagined that having Ross participate would be so nerve-racking!

As the couples left, there was a general air of relief and much laughter, especially from the husbands who had discovered that participating in the birth of their child could be a meaningful experience. Leia gave a sigh of satisfaction, tidied the room, turned out the lights, and locked up. It had been a long day, but somehow the thought of her empty house waiting held no appeal. She pondered this mystery as she walked toward her car. She almost didn't notice Ross waiting beside his red sport car.

When he pushed away from the side of his car, she came to a startled halt under the glare of the street lamp.

"Ross? Did you forget something?"

"Just wanted to make sure you got home safely."

She felt a surge of pleasure at his consideration. There was nothing that warmed a woman's heart like the old-fashioned courtesy of a gentleman. "Well, thanks," she said, then looked past him. "Pamela?"

"Got a ride with a friend. I'll follow you home, okay?"

"I appreciate it, but it's not necessary," she said warmly.

"Don't argue, Leia. Let's go."

Leia gave a little shrug of acquiescence. There was no use tangling with this stubborn Tennessean. In a manner of minutes she had pulled her sedan into her drive and climbed out. Ross parked behind her, unfolding his long length out of the low-slung car. Leia waited for him, rubbing her neck absently.

"Thank you again," she said.

Ross peered narrowly at her through the darkness. "Hey, are you all right?"

"I'm just tired, I guess." And lonely. And wishing things could be different, her brain whispered.

Ross placed his hands on her shoulders and began to massage her tense muscles. Leia felt her tension melting under the magic of his touch.

"Would you like to go for a ride? It'll blow the cobwebs away and relax you. You'll just get depressed if you're alone right now."

"Oh, really, doctor?" Leia's voice was amused.

"Yes, really, nurse. Come on, it's a good way to forget your troubles." He grinned appealingly. "I've been told more than once that I'm just what the doctor ordered."

Leia gave a rather undignified snort of laughter. Never had she met anyone so self-confident about his own charm and attraction! "Go for a ride?" she scoffed lightly. "With you? In that?" She pointed a disdainful finger at his car.

"What's the matter with my car?" he demanded, hands on hips.

"I know your type—speed demon in the air and on the ground!"

"Ma'am, you are dealing with a highly trained individual. Have no fear!"

"Yes, but is it safe?"

"Which, me or the car?" He leered playfully. "You'll just have to wait to find out."

He hustled her around to the passenger side and had her seated before she knew how it had happened. Leia couldn't help but laugh. Just being around him made her feel good! A tiny voice warned that she was playing with fire, but she ignored it, deciding suddenly, against all good sense, that a ride was just what she needed.

Ross got in, sensing that he had won by the indulgent

curve of her shapely lips. The powerful engine roared into life, and he reversed, then sent the sleek machine hurtling through the night.

The air was barely cool and it whipped through the open windows, tangling Leia's hair and carrying her cares away. Ross's occasional comments demanded only desultory answers, and before she realized it she had begun to relax. He followed the curve of Pensacola Bay, then drove over the light-spangled expanse of the Three Mile Bridge into Gulf Breeze and across the toll bridge to Pensacola Beach proper.

The summer shops were closed and there was little activity along the strip. In a moment they were through the town and streaking down the deserted, arrow-straight highway toward the community of Navarre Beach thirty miles away. The white outline of sand dunes rose to the right, then dropped off to the pounding, lacy rush of surf, silver in the starlight.

"Feeling better?" Ross asked.

"Hmm. You know, for a fighter jock you've got a pretty good head on your shoulders," Leia remarked. She touched his arm, feeling the hard, sinewy muscles beneath her fingertips. "Thanks, Ross. You were right, I feel very relaxed now."

He covered her hand with his and squeezed. "Anything for a lady." He pulled into a paved turnaround near a park facility and nodded toward the beach. "Would you like to walk?"

"Sure."

They crossed the narrow dune, the white sand shifting under their feet, the remains of the sea oat fronds clacking in the wind. Ross caught her hand to steady her, then kept it. They walked along the water's edge, hands clasped like school chums, laughing over the antics of the tiny white sand crabs that skittered out of their way. The crash of the surf was a loud, rhythmic pounding that seemed to match the beat of Leia's heart. After a while, by unspoken consent, they turned and started back. The salt-laden breeze blew in Leia's face, and she shivered.

"Cold?" he asked.

"Just a little."

He draped his arm over her shoulders, tugging her close so that their hips touched as they matched steps. "I've got a jacket in the car. I should have given it to you. Sorry."

"I'm all right." She was faintly breathless, and it wasn't entirely due to the physical exertion of walking in the sand. They paused at the water's edge across the dune from the car and watched the waves tumble and roll to the shore.

"Sometimes I come out here alone, just to walk," she said softly.

"You, too?" His arm tightened, and her head rested on his shoulder.

Leia sighed in contentment. She felt wonderfully peaceful, secure, and protected, in perfect rapport with Ross. She pushed away the niggling warnings that were screaming in her mind. Just for right now, at this very moment, she would enjoy the emotional warmth of his presence. She knew it could never be real, but the fantasy was too sweet to give up just yet.

"I love the sea," she murmured dreamily.

"Some are just drawn to it."

A thought wandered across her consciousness. "Is that why you chose the Navy?"

He chuckled. "No. I joined the Navy to fly jets."

A chill raced along her nerve endings, not from the breezy night but from the unwelcome intrusion of reality. Some men seemed to be driven by forces even they could not fully understand. She thought of her father, Stephen, Mitch, Ross, and his compatriots: driven by a need to soar weightless, to control a hurtling piece of machinery as it sliced the blue skies, as if somehow their skill and daring made them more than other, lesser men. They never questioned the price to be paid, no matter how costly to themselves or their loved ones.

Leia pulled away, the fantasy disappearing. "I—I think we'd better go."

"What happened?" Ross's voice held puzzlement. "What did I say?"

"Nothing. It's late, that's all."

"It was that about flying, wasn't it?" he asked roughly. "You have to understand, Leia. That's what I do. It's what I *am.*"

"I understand," she said miserably. "But I've told you before—"

"I know, I know! You won't get involved! And I told you it's too late for that! Can't you see what's happening?" He caught her arms, spun her into the curve of his body to protect her from the sandy wind, and looked down into her startled blue-green eyes.

"Ross, please!"

"Can't you tell how hard I'm trying?" he growled fiercely. "I'm trying to give you room and time, but I want you so badly it's driving me out of my mind!"

"Don't try to feed me a line, flyboy," she said, but her voice was shaky, her thoughts confused.

His sharp, angry expletive shocked her. Then his mouth covered hers in a bruising, sensual kiss that sent her senses reeling. When he lifted his head, they were both breathing heavily.

"You'd have known a long time ago if that was all I wanted," he said through gritted teeth. A new tension came over him and she sensed his hesitation, felt the subtle difference in the pressure of his hands. His voice was low and husky, almost pleading. "Can't you tell I'm falling in love with you?"

"Don't say that!" she gasped.

"I'm just a country boy, Leia. I'm not very good at hiding my feelings."

"Oh, Ross!" she cried, swallowing hard on threatening tears. "I didn't want this."

"Well, you got it."

He looked down at her stricken expression, and his features softened with tenderness. He gathered her close, threading his fingers through her silky tangles to press her cheek against his shoulder. Convulsive shudders raced over her, and he made little soothing sounds against her temple.

"All right, Leia. I'll back off," he said at last. "But that doesn't mean I'm giving up. You'll find we Tennesseans can be damned stubborn folks."

"I don't want to hurt you, Ross."

"You won't."

"I don't want you to hurt me."

"I won't."

She swallowed and smiled, amused anew at his unwavering confidence. "Don't you ever get tired of beating your head against a brick wall?"

"Ladybird, when that happens, I just fly over it."

It seemed to Leia that the next few weeks were like a roller-coaster ride. She was up when Ross was in town, down when he was gone with his team to yet another Blue Angels exhibition. He had the disconcerting habit of popping into her life when she least expected, whisking her away to some activity, taking her acceptance for granted or at least never giving her a chance to refuse his invitations.

They visited art galleries and museums, fished off the public pier for grouper, jogged together on the city trails, even went golfing on the lush course at the naval air station. Somehow Ross made being with him such a sheer pleasure that Leia couldn't find it in herself to deny his spontaneous entertainments, knowing that all too soon he'd be flying off to another location across the country. He was always in attendance with Pamela at the childbirth classes and took to buying them both coffee afterward and listening indulgently to discussions of baby clothes and nurseries.

He was careful to keep their tenuous relationship on a friendly basis, never pressuring Leia for anything more than she was willing to give, and for that she was grateful. She stopped trying to analyze what she felt for him, consigning those confusing thoughts to the back of her mind. His breezy ways, unfailing good humor, and thoughtful consideration of her every whim made her simply relax and enjoy the ride. It was nice to be coddled, catered to, and admired. Leia came to accept this interlude, content with the thought that she could enjoy his company with no strings, knowing that when at some point he decided to "ship out," they would both have kept their promises not to hurt each other.

It was really best this way, she decided, and took joyously what the gods had sent.

The bell on the door of The Gingerbread Shop jangled merrily. Leia thumbtacked the last black bat to the Halloween window display and turned around to find herself looking straight into Ross's smiling hazel eyes.

"Ross, you're back!" she said warmly.

"Hi, ladybird. Yeah, we had clear weather all the way from Canada." His eyes gleamed at the vibrant picture she made in her green-and-gold plaid blouse and kelly green slacks. Lord, he'd missed her!

"You must be tired." She licked her lips. References to his flying always tied her stomach in knots. She knew it was childish, but it was easier to ignore his career altogether, to pretend it just didn't exist. That way she didn't have to deal with it.

"Is that you, Commander?" Elizabeth's frowsy topknot poked out of the storage room door.

"Yes, ma'am, Miss Elizabeth," Ross answered with a grin. He stuck his hands into his pockets and rocked back on the heels of his shoes.

"About time, young man. She's been mooning around here all day, lonesome as a polecat. Why don't you get her out of my hair?"

"Elizabeth, really!" Leia admonished her, blushing. "I've got to finish tagging those dresses."

"That can wait. Go have some fun. Go on, you two, get out of here!" Elizabeth shooed them away, mumbling to herself. "Can't a body get any peace and quiet?"

"You mean I can have you all to myself?" Ross asked Leia, one dark eyebrow cocked inquiringly.

"Well—yes!"

"Then what are we waiting for?"

Laughing, Leia allowed herself to be hustled off to his car. "Where are we going?"

"I want you to see my place. It's great this time of day."

Leia settled back with a sigh of contentment, satisfied to bask in the glow of his company.

It was a perfect day, one of those sunny, pleasant fall days that seem all the more precious because the gray, rainy winter was soon to set in. Ross stopped to pick up a pizza, then drove through Warrington past the naval air station toward Perdido Key. He turned into a secluded, pine-tree-lined drive, and before Leia knew it, they had pulled up at a zigzag row of townhouses with the sparkling waters of Perdido Bay just beyond.

Leia looked around with appreciative eyes. "Oh, Ross, this is lovely."

He grinned, juggling his keys and the pizza box as he unlocked the door and ushered her inside. The townhouse was on two stories, the kitchen and living area downstairs opening onto a large wooden deck. A spiral staircase led upstairs. The furnishings were large and comfortable, in warm earth tones, and the place was meticulously tidy. Only a plastic-wrapped hanger of clean uniforms lay draped across the back of a dining chair to indicate that someone did indeed live here.

"Well, what do you think?" he asked, depositing the pizza on the kitchen counter.

Leia couldn't suppress a smile of amazement. "You're so —neat!"

Ross laughed and rummaged in the cabinet for glasses. "That's one thing the military will do for you. That and the fact that I'm not here very much. But I like it. It's quiet and sometimes I really need to get away from the crowds for a little private time."

"Then I'm intruding."

"Don't be dumb, Leia. I don't invite just anybody here, you know." He passed her the filled glasses and gestured toward the sliding glass door. "Let's eat outside, okay?"

They stuffed themselves with pizza and enjoyed the quiet lap of the water, watching the sun sink lower and lower like a flaming ball until it disappeared into the bay.

Their conversation trailed off, but Leia didn't mind. In fact, she enjoyed the easy silences as much as Ross's teasing banter. She wiped her fingers on her napkin and glanced at Ross. He was tired, she thought. And small wonder, having flown from Canada after a grueling weekend show schedule. He seemed a bit preoccupied, and she didn't want to interrupt whatever thoughts distracted him. She wrapped her arm around the post supporting the deck railing and watched a flock of gulls diving into the rapidly darkening waters of the bay.

"You're awfully quiet." Ross was next to her, his arm braced on the post behind her back. His face was close to hers, and his warm breath moved the tendrils of hair at her temple.

"So are you," she murmured.

He glanced out over the water. "It'll be winter soon. My two years as a Blue Angel are just about over. The new pilots have been named. By the end of November I'll be history."

"I didn't know." Leia swallowed. Here it comes, she thought. What she had been waiting for all along. It was time to say farewell, the old brush off, the it-was-fun-while-it-lasted spiel. She knew it was inevitable; it was what she wanted, she told herself fiercely. But she was stunned by the anguish that wrenched at her soul.

He continued, his voice low. "It's unofficial, but I'll probably end up at Miramar for eight or nine months of training before I go back to the boat. You know our last show is in November here in Pensacola. After that I'll be out of here."

Leia closed her eyes on a white flash of pain, then blinked wide, gasping at his next words.

"When I go, Leia, I want to take you with me. As my wife."

CHAPTER FIVE

This can't be happening, Leia thought wildly. Little green men with red tails waved their pointed caps and gamboled crazily on her nerve endings. She felt faint and dizzy and heard Ross's deep voice as if from a great, hollow distance.

"I know it's fast," he said, leaning over her. His large palm cupped the gentle curve of her cheek. "But I know what I want. I love you, Leia."

Leia felt a surge of sheer panic. Then his mouth covered hers, and she had no choice but to melt into him, to give herself up to the unmitigated madness of the moment. She whimpered deep in her throat, and Ross answered with a hungry male groan. His tongue probed, tasted, savored the essence of her mouth, rendering her boneless, jointless.

His hands splayed across her back and traveled the supple carved ridge of her spine, pulling her hips into the cradle of his thighs and letting her feel the power of his desire. Leia shuddered, the melting honey of passion dissolving her will. Her fingers curled into the fabric of his shirt, and she tasted the heat of his mouth. His knuckles brushed the full curve of her breast and sanity returned with the chill of an icy Arctic breath. She tore her lips away.

"No, Ross. Stop." She choked out the words, pushing against his massive chest.

"Oh, Leia! God, I want you!" His breathing was ragged.

A thousand different emotions crashed together within Leia. Unable to stand the turmoil, she wrenched free of Ross's embrace, whirling, then staggering to a halt. She pressed the heels of her hands against her stinging eyelids, dragging in one shaky breath after another in an effort to get control of herself. Cleansing breath, she told herself firmly, as if she were one of her own Lamaze students. Relax, ride the pain. It'll pass.

"Leia? What is it, honey?" Ross's hands lightly touched her shoulders. She flinched, backing away from him, her eyes wide and shadowed.

"Please, Ross," she begged huskily. "You're making it so hard."

His lips quirked upward. "What's so hard about getting married? People do it everyday."

"I—I can't marry you." Her tone was tortured, raspy with despair and remorse for inflicting the hurt she could not help. She saw the burning gold light in his eyes and looked away. "I tried to warn you . . . I think you'd better take me home."

She moved to the door, but he caught her elbow in a viselike grip. "Wait a minute! What did you think all this was leading to?" He was truly puzzled.

"Nowhere! You knew it and I knew it! Just some fun until it was over. A few laughs, no regrets." Her voice rose in panic. "We weren't supposed to fall in love!"

"Well, I don't know how to make myself any clearer, Leia," he snapped.

"I told you. I told you! You're a pilot and—"

"You're not being rational about this, Leia. I know you had a bad experience in the past, but that's over! I'm highly trained in what I do. I don't take chances in the air." He gave her a little shake. "Dammit, I'm one of the best! If the

83

Navy trusts me not to kill myself and take down a multimillion-dollar aircraft, why can't you?"

"I know it's not rational!" she cried. "My head tells me all those things, but my gut tells me that if—if I love you, you'll die, too! I can't take that kind of chance again!"

"People die every day! What's not to say I'll walk out of here and into the path of a truck? Or get struck by lightning? I've got a better chance of dying in bed than in an airplane!"

"All right!" she screamed, the first tear slipping from the corner of her eye. "I'm afraid. I'm a coward! I admit it! But I can't help myself!"

Ross's voice grew gentle. "Baby, baby. I'll help you."

"You can't. No one can. I look at you in that crisp blue uniform, see those pilot's wings, and I'm terrified. God help me! I'm so scared that someday you'll crash and burn just like Mitch! Don't you understand?"

His expression was stony. "Sure, I understand. You'll let a dead man stand between us—between what we might have together. You're running away again, just like you did the night we met!" he accused angrily. "Dammit, I know you love me! Why can't you admit it?"

Ashamed at her lack of courage, confused about her true feelings, and battling the terror of the past, Leia lashed out in desperation.

"You're so sure of yourself!" she sneered, jerking free of his hand. She wiped the tears from her eyes, taking anger as her defense. "Why do I have to love you? Just because you want me to? You're so used to things going your way, but not this time, Ross! I'm the only one who can decide what's right for me!"

"Then I beg your pardon all to hell, Ms. McKenzie!" His voice was scathing with his contempt. "Go ahead and crawl into that little hole of yours and maybe the world won't notice you. But it's not because you're afraid I'll *die*, but because you're too scared to *live!*"

Leia blanched, struck by the truth in his words. She turned abruptly, stalked through the townhouse and grabbed her purse in a blind rush to escape.

"Where the hell do you think you're going?" Ross roared, catching up with her.

"Home." She swallowed and chanced a look at his enraged features. "Please?"

Cursing under his breath, Ross grabbed his keys in a swipe of barely restrained violence. He gritted his teeth. "Let's go."

Leia blinked rapidly, willing herself not to give in to the stinging rush of threatening tears. She swallowed again and stared off into the distance. Her voice was strained. "I—I never wanted to hurt you. I'm sorry."

He ran an agitated hand through his hair and gazed up at the ceiling. The long breath he drew in flared his nostrils, and Leia saw the telltale bob of his Adam's apple. "I know, Leia. That's what makes it so damned frustrating. I have no one to blame but myself."

Leia's heart twisted at the raw pain in his voice. She followed him to the car silently, in agony for him and for herself, knowing that she'd never see him again, and knowing that it was the only right—the only smart—thing to do. And wishing that the gods had allowed two fools a little more time in paradise.

"Trick or treat!" A pint-size green-faced ghoul yelled the familiar greeting and was joined in chorus by the Sugar Plum Fairy, a black-robed ax-wielding headsman, and a pretty fair imitation of Hulk Hogan.

"Oh, my goodness! What a scary bunch of goblins!" Leia exclaimed, smiling at the group on her tiny porch. She dropped handfuls of wrapped candy into each outstretched plastic pumpkin and rumpled paper bag.

"Gee, thanks!"

"Yeah, thanks!"

"Happy Halloween!"

Leia smiled and waved. The neighborhood was alive with all sorts of spooks and zany characters, and she was having as much fun as the children.

It was the first time anything had pleased her since she had broken up with Ross. No, that wasn't right, she thought. You couldn't break up with someone you'd never gotten together with in the first place. One more regret to add to the list. But then lists were never very good comfort when you were downright miserable!

She pushed the door closed and rubbed her aching neck, remembering how Ross's sensitive touch could so easily massage her tension away. Damn! Why did every little thing have to remind her of him? It wasn't enough that her dreams were filled with him and visions of speeding aircraft, or that Elizabeth looked at her with silent, accusing disapproval. No, there was a gaping emptiness in her life, in her heart. She hadn't even been aware of how he'd carved himself a place in her daily existence until he was gone. She had done what she had to do, out of sheer self-preservation. But why did surviving have to be so painful?

The doorbell rang again. Leia set a smile in place and opened the door.

"Trick or treat!" The tiny witch in black robes and a tall pointed hat shrieked excitedly. She clutched the neck of the tall pirate who carried her easily in his strong arms.

Leia froze, and her heart drummed a tattoo. It was Biddie and her "uncle" Ross. His brown hair was covered with a red bandanna, and he wore a plastic eye patch and an assortment of scars and blemishes evidently drawn on in eyebrow pencil with great abandon by a childish hand. What she could see of his expression was curiously solemn. He looked ridiculous, handsome, *wonderful!*

"Oh, my goodness," Leia said, forcing her attention back to the child. She dumped handfuls of candy into her bag. "It's Bridget the Witch, isn't it?"

"Aww! You knew!" Biddie wailed.

"Yes, but I've never seen a spookier witch," Leia hastened to reassure her. She gave an exaggerated shudder. "I'm scared to death!"

"Uncle Ross said you would be," Biddie said smugly.

Leia shot a look at the pirate and swallowed with difficulty. "Your uncle Ross knows me pretty well," she murmured, aware that there was more than one interpretation to be made of those innocuous words. "Would you like to come in and see my jack-o'-lantern?"

"Could I? Swell!" Biddie wriggled out of Ross's arms and scurried inside to inspect the grinning pumpkin face shining in Leia's front window.

Leia bit her lip and gestured awkwardly. "Come on in."

"Just for a minute," Ross replied, following her just inside the doorway. "I promised Pamela I wouldn't keep the little witch out too long. She didn't feel up to the walk herself."

"That's awfully nice of you," Leia said softly. "Not every uncle would agree to . . . to . . ." She smiled and pointed helplessly at his get-up.

"Biddie's idea. I have this sudden urge to say 'Shiver me timbers!' and 'Avast, me hearties!' "

She laughed. "Do your best to resist it, Commander!"

He leaned back against the wall and raised his eye patch. "So," he said, his voice low, "how have you been?"

"Okay. And you?" She glanced away, her tone tremulous.

"Not so good." He caught her chin with his thumb and

lifted her face. "You don't lie very well. Now, tell me the truth."

Leia's blue-green eyes flashed wide in surprise, and she took a shaky breath. "It's been hell," she admitted.

"Good. Very good." His words held satisfaction, but his hazel eyes blazed with a hungry, golden fire.

"It doesn't change anything," she whispered.

"It's time we made it change." He bent toward her.

"You gonna kiss her, Uncle Ross?" piped a high voice behind them.

Leia jumped, and Ross chuckled at her blush. "Not right now, Biddie," he answered the child, smiling affectionately. "Are you ready to do some more trick-or-treating?"

"Yeah!"

Ross gave Leia a look that melted her bones. "I'll be back," he promised.

Over an hour later the doorbell again rang with an imperative peal. The tiny spooks and goblins had disappeared indoors to devour their treats, but Leia had spent the time pacing and lecturing herself. She must be firm and unemotional, must try to make Ross see once and for all. . . . The thought made her feel like running, taking the car keys and driving to the beach, anyplace. But Ross had accused her of running away before. She would stay and deal with the problem like an adult, and they could at least part friends.

She squared her shoulders and opened the door.

Ross burst in with all the power of his forceful personality, staring at her hard and backing her into the house. He had shed his bandanna and eye patch but still sported the results of Biddie's artistic endeavors on his face. He kicked the door shut behind him with a resounding slam.

"Woman, you and I have got to have a serious talk!" he announced.

"We do?" Leia squeaked. She backed away cautiously,

intimidated by his size, his blatant masculinity, and most of all, her own singing response. She closed her eyes for an instant to fight the dangerous jangling of her nerves.

"Yes, we do! I figured it out."

"What?"

"We were so busy concentrating on each other, we forgot to do anything about our basic problem."

"We did?" She was properly confused.

He crowded her against the wall and grasped her shoulders. "Yes, we did. And that's finding a way to rid you of this understandable reluctance to be around pilots. What we need is a serious campaign to reeducate you!"

"Reeducate?" she echoed, dazed.

"Yes, you see—"

"Ross?" she interrupted, shaking her head. A little helpless laugh escaped her. "I'm sorry, but I just can't talk seriously to a pirate with a scar and a wart on his nose!"

He touched his cheek. "Oh, I forgot all about it."

She licked the tip of her finger and gently scrubbed at the mark on the side of his nose. "Don't worry, I think you're washable."

Ross became strangely tense. He caught her wrist in an iron clasp, then slowly, slowly let his lips trail along her sensitive wrist, across her palm, then nibbled on the tip of her finger before taking it in his mouth and sucking gently.

Leia gasped, and a little moan escaped her. Shivers of sensuality crawled across her skin and an inner fire blazed, dazzling her senses. "Ross!" she cried raggedly and lifted her mouth in blind appeal.

He crushed her to him, his mouth seeking, finding the sweetness of her lips. She fit in his arms so perfectly. How could she not feel the rightness of it? He kissed her cheekbone, her temple, the delicate shell of her ear. He felt the answering tremors that matched the shaking of his hands as he molded her to him. He fingered the cords of her neck, breathing in her fragrance, his words a tumbling litany of desire and hope.

"We can work it out, Leia. I know we can. I rushed you. I'm sorry. Give us a chance. You've got what it takes."

"Ross, Ross!" Her fingers stroked frantically at the nape of his neck, threading through his hair. His name was an entreaty, her tear-filled voice near despair. "What are we going to *do?*"

He took a deep breath, willing himself to calmness. This was too important to blow with a few kisses and some half-thought-out explanations. He had to make her see. He had to make her want to try.

He led her to the sofa, pulled her down beside him, and gently tucked a red-gold curl behind her ear. Her mouth was swollen from his kisses and it was all he could do not to take her in his arms and make her his right there on the living room couch. Instead he traced the bone in her jaw and took another deep breath.

"You care for me," he said quietly. It was not a question.

"Yes, of course, I care, but . . ." She lifted her hands helplessly.

"Look, I'm not going to try to force a commitment you're not ready to give, but I think—I hope—that if we go about this logically, we can come to a compromise, or at least come to an understanding about my career that will alleviate some of your fears. Maybe then you can give me the answer I want."

"But how? I'm not sure there's anything that can be done," she said, her voice quavering.

He twined his fingers through hers, then held them tight. "I'm not going to paint you a rosy picture about the way things might be. A Navy career can be a demanding, brutal mistress. There're the separations, the periodic reassignments, and a thousand other things that make it a unique, challenging life. But it can be a good life, Leia—if the commitment is there, if the love is there between two people who want to make it work."

"It's not the way of life that worries me. I'm an Air Force brat, remember? If you were just a sailor . . ."

"But I'm not. I'm a pilot. I love my country and I love to fly. I get real satisfaction out of what I do."

"Have—have you ever considered another career?"

He shook his head. "Not since I got my wings. Someday . . . I don't know. I look down the road to retirement and I think about going back to Tennessee. I could do other things—public relations, business, even politics. But that's a long way off. This is what I do now—and I'm damned good at it."

"But that doesn't change anything." Leia held her hand against her middle as if something painful gnawed at her vitals.

"I don't think you're giving yourself enough credit. You're a tough lady." He saw her dubious expression and sighed. "Look, it's been a long time since Mitch was killed, hasn't it?"

"Seven years."

"You've grown and matured in that time. Hell, I'll be the first to admit that I was pretty reckless my first years in the air. But you don't last long that way, and I don't just mean by cashing it in, either. You wash out, or get kicked out. I'm a lot mellower than I was ten years ago. I *want* to keep my precious hide in one piece!"

Leia laughed gently. "Thank God for that!"

He grinned, then sobered again. "And your brother. He died in troubled times, but we're at peace now. And if we ever went to war, I'd be on the front lines whether I was in a jet or not. That's the kind of man I am."

91

"I realize that." It was her turn to be painfully honest. "It's those wonderful, strong things in you that are so attractive to me. They're also the things that scare me."

"I want you to face your fears and put them to rest, Leia. For me. For *us*."

"How?"

"I want you to see me fly a program. I want you to watch me fly with the Blues and see for yourself that I know what I'm doing."

Leia paled, and a cold sweat broke out on her forehead. "I —I don't know if I'm up to that, Ross."

"Please, honey. Our next performance is at the naval air station in New Orleans. That's only a few hours away by car. You could come for the weekend, see the show, and maybe we could even do the French Quarter afterward." His smile became teasing, persuasive. "You know you'll only have a couple more chances to see me do my stuff!"

"You're just an old show-off, huh?" Her voice was shaky.

"I love the limelight! Seriously, it could be the first step. Won't you try—for us?"

Leia's throat worked convulsively, and the blood roared in her ears. Could she do it? She looked into Ross's earnest, handsome face and felt a surge of tenderness for the giving, compassionate person he was. A nameless emotion filled her, something she didn't dare examine too closely. She knew that she had to take the chance. Slowly she nodded her agreement.

"That's my girl!" Ross beamed and blew out the breath he'd been holding. "And I want you to get to know my friends and their wives, and the other team members. You'll see we're just folks doing a job. If you meet the wives, you can see how they deal with things every day."

"All right, Ross." This was something she could do.

"How about tomorrow night? The Boss invited some of us

over to see the Army-Navy game he recorded on the VCR last weekend. Just a casual get-together."

"Fine." Leia lay back on the couch, feeling as though she had been wrung out with a wringer. She gazed at Ross and suddenly giggled.

"What's so funny?"

"You. Looking so pleased with yourself—with all that gunk still on your face!"

He gave a mock growl and leapt for her, tussling with her until they were both breathless and laughing. He pinned her flat on the couch, and his lips were merely a breath away. Their eyes met, and smiles died.

"You know," he said, his voice low and husky, "I kind of liked the way you washed it off before."

"I could do better."

"Show me."

A little shyly she lifted her head, softly kissing the smeared pencil scar on his cheek. The tip of her tongue flicked out, delicately licking at the mark, making a little rasping sound against the stubble of his beard. She moved to the next mark, and Ross's dark lashes lowered. There was a low rumble in his throat.

"Is it working?" he asked.

"Not especially. Do you care?"

"Nope."

"I didn't think so," she said with a laugh, then moved to his lips, knowing full well that no makeup marred their sensual line. She lightly outlined his mouth, sucked gently at the corners, but when she nibbled at the lower curve, his growl became real. He took over her game with one dashing charge, capturing her elusive lips and kissing her breathless, demanding no less than surrender, and then throwing himself on her tender mercies.

When at last he pulled away, they were both gasping,

bodies tuned in perfect accord. Leia was faintly puzzled by Ross's restraint, but she knew in her heart that without it, she would have followed his lead to the only possible conclusion. And whether or not her heart and mind was ready, her body ached for him.

Ross raked a shaking hand over his face and tugged his ear. "Jeez! You never fail to surprise me, Leia."

"You still need to wash your face." She sat up, brushing back her hair.

"I'm thinking in terms of a cold shower right now."

She laughed, but it was a bit uncertain. "I'm surprised, too. I've always wanted to make love to a pirate." She fidgeted with a loose thread in the sofa upholstery. His hand covered hers, and she looked up into his eyes, which had gone a warm, rich brown.

"You'll get your chance. When we're both ready. I don't want to rush you into a physical relationship only to find out I've made another mistake. Do you understand?"

"I take back all the nasty things I ever thought about oversexed fighter pilots."

"You'll get the opportunity to do some hands-on research, and that's a promise, ladybird." He grinned and dropped a quick kiss on her lips. "In the meantime, I've got a date with that shower! Pick you up at seven tomorrow, okay?"

"Okay." She followed him to the door. "Watch out for boogeymen."

His hand cupped her cheek. "We're going to chase them away—together."

It didn't matter whether you were Navy or civilian, Leia thought in amusement. At a party like this the men always seemed to congregate in the den and the women in the kitchen. A ragged chorus of male voices sounded from the

94

direction of the den, where a TV announcer spouted colorful commentary about the Army-Navy football game.

"Just listen to that," said Melinda Lohman, the Boss's vivacious spouse, with a laugh. "As if they didn't know the score already!"

"Who won?" Pamela Anderson asked, reaching for another chip from a bowl on the buffet laid out on the kitchen table.

"Would you believe I don't even know?" Melinda asked.

Leia joined in the general laughter of wives and dates. Despite her earlier trepidations, and Ross's apparent abandonment of her to the kitchen contingency, she was enjoying herself. The gathering at the Lohmans' included a couple of Ross's teammates, assorted Navy personnel, neighbors, and the team's flight surgeon, Peter Neely. Leia and the doctor had had a long discussion regarding the nurse-midwife's role in modern medicine before the game had garnered his attention. Now the women had retreated to the kitchen to discuss children, schools, fashions, and the trials and tribulations of base life—all things Leia could easily relate to.

"I think those men have talked football and planes long enough," Melinda said. She grabbed a tray of snacks from the table. "Let's see if they'll let us join the party. Leia, would you and Pam fill some more glasses for me?"

Leia joined Pamela at the sink, working with a bag of crushed ice and some fresh glasses. They were alone in the kitchen.

"Ross deserted you?" Pamela asked with an impish grin.

"It would look that way, but I don't mind. I wouldn't dream of interrupting such an important ball game," Leia replied. "Besides, everyone's been so nice."

"It's a good group. Lots of give-and-take, but some real deep feelings of friendship lie under all that joking around."

"I think that's what Ross wants me to understand."

Pamela wiped her hands on a dish towel and looked at Leia, a concerned expression crossing her lovely face. "Am I wrong, or are things getting serious between the two of you?"

"Well—maybe," Leia said, her voice faltering.

"I'm so glad," Pamela said warmly. "Ross is such a special person. He needs someone who'll really appreciate him."

Leia bit her lip. "I do care about him, Pamela, but it's not easy for me to ignore the dangers involved in his career. I'm working on it, but . . ." She shrugged. "How do you deal with it?"

Pamela sighed and placed a protective hand on her rounded belly. "It's not easy sometimes," she admitted. "I'd be lying to say I never worry about Webb. He's in the Mediterranean now, and the Mideast is such a powder keg. Anything could happen."

"That's the kind of thing that scares me, as well as the programs that Ross flies with the Blue Angels. I saw enough air shows as a kid to give me the willies for a lifetime, but he wants me to come to New Orleans to watch them fly."

"Are you going?"

"I said I would."

"These men are different," Pamela said slowly. "They just don't know what fear is. Flying is number one with them, and they concentrate fully on it. It's when they don't that you should start worrying. It takes a special kind of woman to accept that."

"I know," Leia said miserably. "I don't want to hurt Ross, but I'm not sure I have that in me."

"When Webb was in flight school, we had a friend whose wife actually got physically sick every time he went up. He washed out. The wrong kind of woman can be deadly."

"Why aren't you afraid, Pamela?"

"I didn't say I wasn't," she replied gently. She touched Leia's shoulder. "I had as many—or more—doubts as you do now. But when it came down to being part of Webb's life or not . . . well, you can see what I chose." She patted her tummy and smiled.

"You're braver than I am."

"No, but sometimes you make bargains in life. You have to accept the risks to get what you want."

Leia mulled over Pamela's words as they carried the pitcher and glasses into the den. Would she ever have that kind of courage? She didn't know, but seeing Ross sprawled in a chair, watching the ball game with his chin resting on his fist, looking so handsome and virile that part of her twisted with yearning, she knew she had to find out.

"Hey, you." She nudged Ross's shoulder, smiling down at him and offering a frosty glass. "I didn't know you were so into football."

"Hmm? Oh, thanks, hon." He took the glass and hooked her around the waist with his arm, pulling her down to sit on the arm of the chair. Around them, the other guests cheered the feats of a Navy tight end on the television screen. "I haven't been very good company, have I?"

"Never mind. We ladies have enjoyed the visit." She watched him down half the glass in two gulps. She frowned slightly. Her instincts went suddenly to alert. Ross's lids looked puffy, and he seemed flushed. "Are you all right?"

Ross rubbed his eyes and grimaced. "Actually I don't feel too well. I think I'm coming down with a cold. First one I've had in years."

She placed a professional hand on his forehead. "You're feverish!"

"Now, ladybird, don't hover," he admonished with a drawl. "I'm okay."

"You ought to be home in bed."

His eyes glowed and his lips quirked upward. "Why, Leia, what a good idea!"

"Alone!"

"Spoilsport." He shifted his long length in the chair and stifled a groan. "Christ, I'm stiff. Maybe it wouldn't be a bad idea to call it a night, if you don't mind."

"Of course."

They made their farewells, and while Leia was thanking Melinda Lohman, she noticed that Ross had a word with Pete Neely. The men disappeared for a moment; then Ross was at her side again, shaking hands with the Boss.

Outside, Leia could not contain her curiosity.

"Did you speak with the doctor?"

Ross held her elbow and walked her to where the red 'Vette sat snugly against the curb. "Yeah. Quit worrying. He gave me something from his bag to keep my head clear." He pulled a bottle of tablets out of his shirt pocket. "You get stopped-up ears at thirty thousand feet and believe me, you know it!"

"You need something to reduce the fever, too. Have you got anything at home?"

"You are such a worrywart! Cool it, McKenzie. It's just a cold, for heaven's sake!" Annoyance sharpened the edge of his voice.

"But—"

Leia broke off suddenly. Ross's hand tightened on her elbow and his steps faltered. He shook his head and blinked, then rubbed his eyes. He took another step and swayed against the side of the car.

"Ross? What is it?" Her concern turned to alarm when she saw him pale beneath his tan. He released her elbow and swayed again, this time catching himself with both hands braced on the hood of the car.

"Just a little—dizzy," he muttered. He swallowed harshly on a wave of sudden nausea.

"I'll go get Pete."

"No!" Jesus! He couldn't be sick this late in the season. He had to fly. He gritted his teeth to try to stop the spinning scenery. "Conner."

"What? What can I do?" She supported his weight with her flimsy strength.

"Here." He thrust the car keys into her hand. "Try to get me home."

CHAPTER SIX

Leia didn't like fast cars. She didn't like to ride in them, and she especially didn't like to drive them. But during the nightmare ride to Ross's place she gave silent thanks for the Corvette's powerful engine, getting a kind of perverse pleasure out of her ability to master this demon of hers when Ross needed it most.

She glanced at him, slumped in the passenger seat, his eyes covered by one hand. He was quiet—too quiet—and there was a nasty grayish tinge to his skin.

"Pull over."

"We're almost there." She swung into the tree-lined lane that led to his apartment.

"For God's sake, Leia!" he said with a groan, a hint of desperation in his voice. "Pull over—now."

Leia saw his jaw clench in a spasm and braked sharply, pulling the low-slung car over on the grassy shoulder. Ross was out of the car and heading unsteadily for the shelter of the tall pines before the wheels stopped moving. Leia was poised to follow him, but he reappeared within minutes, weaving his way toward the car. He dropped into the seat and sighed with the utter exhaustion of someone who has just been thoroughly sick.

"Sorry," he muttered.

"Are you all right?"

"My head's spinning." He lay his head on the back of the seat and closed his eyes.

Leia put the car into gear. "We'll be home in a minute."

It was no small task getting Ross inside his apartment and up the stairs to the bedroom. Leia had never seen such a swift and severe onslaught of vertigo. It frightened her to see Ross, normally so strong and self-sufficient, reduced to such helplessness. At the same time she felt an overwhelming need to nurture him as best she could, to reverse their positions and take care of him for a change. She got him down on the king-size bed and began to remove his shoes and socks.

"Hey, I'm okay," he protested weakly. "Must have been something I ate."

"Sure. That accounts for the fever and head congestion, too, I suppose," she retorted. "I think I ought to call Pete."

"Hell, no! All I need is to sleep it off."

She sat down beside him on the edge of the bed and frowned. "I don't like this extreme dizziness. My dad suffers from Ménière's syndrome and the symptoms are similar. You can't fly with an inner ear disturbance."

"This isn't anything like that," Ross said defensively. "I just picked up a bug or something. Besides, we aren't scheduled to fly tomorrow anyway. I'll be all right. Look, you take the car and go on home. I'm sorry to end our evening on such a lousy note."

"Don't worry about it." She touched his forehead. "Where do you keep your medicine? I'll get you something for that fever."

He gestured vaguely. "Downstairs, in the kitchen."

"I'll be right back. Don't move."

"Don't worry."

Leia poked around his sparsely supplied kitchen until she found the medicine she wanted and a single bottle of lemon-lime soft drink. She also found a couple of cans of soup and set them out, too. She heard water running in the upstairs bath and tensed, listening for the sound of someone falling, but all she heard was a low groan and the squeak of bedsprings. Filling a tall glass with ice and the soft drink, she climbed the stairs again.

Ross had fallen, fully clothed, onto his stomach across the top of the burgundy corduroy bedspread. Leia gave a little sigh of exasperation and set down the glass on the bedside table. With swift, efficient movements she flung back the spread as far as she could, then pulled his shirt out of the waistband of his slacks. At least she could make him more comfortable.

Ross mumbled something, and she touched his shoulder and rolled him over on the sheets. Her fingers went to work on his shirt buttons.

"I said, what are you doing?" Ross asked, squinting his eyes to look at her.

"Undressing you."

"Just my luck."

She pulled his shirt away, trying not to stare at the whorls of soft dark hair that covered his well-muscled chest, and began to unbuckle his belt. "What about your luck?"

Ross closed his eyes and grimaced wryly. "Got you in my bedroom undressing me, but I'm too wretched to do anything about it."

"Oh, shut up. I'm a nurse. I've seen a man before."

"Wouldn't you know it? Can't even impress you with my gorgeous bod."

Leia laughed softly and shook her head. Even flat on his back, he had enough ego for five men. She gave his hip a pat and he shifted so she could slip his slacks off, revealing dark blue briefs. She allowed herself a split-second to admire him —trim waist, broad shoulders, long legs—and stifled a feminine sigh at his masculine perfection. Controlling her galloping thoughts, she flipped the sheets up and tried to keep her voice businesslike. "Here, take your medicine."

Ross dutifully swallowed the pills, grimacing at the sharp taste of the soda.

"These, too," Leia said, offering him the tablets he'd gotten from the flight surgeon. "Do you feel like some soup or something?"

Ross groaned and fell back on the pillows. His watch glinted on the wrist he threw over his eyes. "You've got a mean streak, woman. Don't mention food. And remind me to beat you later to make up for all these insults to my dignity."

Leia's lips twitched. "Try to get some sleep." She felt his forehead again, as though the medicine could be working already, but really just to touch him. Ross's hand curled around her wrist and he opened a bleary eye.

"Thanks."

"Anytime, flyboy."

She paused at the door and flicked off the light switch. Ross settled into the covers and sighed. She could hear his teeth grinding back another moan, and she hesitated. She couldn't leave him just yet. What if he had another attack?

She went downstairs and put the soup cans away. There was nothing to tidy in the immaculate kitchen, so she wandered around the living area, looking at the bookshelves that contained Ross's awards and mementos, finally settling on the sofa with an aviation magazine. After a while she tiptoed back upstairs to check on him.

He was sleeping, but fitfully, mumbling restlessly in his dreams. His fever didn't seem to be any lower, either. Leia made a decision. She found an extra blanket in the hall closet and prepared herself for a long night.

She made numerous trips up and down those stairs,

103

checking on her patient. At one point Ross roused enough for her to get another dose of medicine down him, but he didn't question her presence, merely rolled over and went back to sleep. Leia was exhausted but gratified when his fever broke sometime in the wee hours. She curled up in her blanket on the sofa and went gratefully to sleep.

The smell of coffee and soft, cheerful whistling woke Leia shortly after dawn. She groaned and reached for her blanket, noticing that a second one had been added at some time. She squeezed her eyes closed and tried to recapture the sweet essence of sleep. Firm, warm lips nuzzled her just behind the ear.

"Wake up, sleepyhead."

"Uh-uh."

A hand delved under the blankets, stroking her back through her rumpled blouse. Teeth nipped delicately at her earlobe, then his hand smoothed around her rib cage and came to rest on her breast. "Time to rise and shine, ladybird."

"Unhand me," she groused. She pushed his searching hand away and struggled to sit up. "You're supposed to be sick."

Ross hunkered down beside the sofa, wearing a blue terry robe. His hair was damp, and he was freshly shaved. His hazel eyes sparkled. "Do I look sick?"

Leia eyed him critically. She felt his cheek, his forehead, but they were cool. "Hmm. How do you feel?"

"Fine. See, I told you all I needed was a good night's sleep."

Leia stretched and arched her spine, grumbling at the stiffness induced by a night on a lumpy couch. "Well, I'm glad somebody got one."

"You should have climbed in with me. There's room in that big bed for two."

Leia laughed. "You weren't *that* sick!"

He grinned and shrugged. "It just doesn't seem fair that you got to take off my clothes and I didn't get to return the favor."

"You'll get your chance," she promised airily, as she flung aside the blankets.

"Yeah? When?" His voice was a husky growl, and he eased up beside her. "How about now?"

Leia's heart pumped double time. She pushed her tangled hair back from her face, and her laugh was shaky. "Are you kidding? Do you realize how sick you were last night? Besides, you're still weak, and I must look like death warmed over!"

"Uh-uh. Lovely and warm and tumbled." His mouth poised, then sipped at her lips with each softly spoken word. He held her in the curve of his arms and looked down into the depths of her turquoise eyes. "I can't tell you how good it made me feel when I found you here this morning. Thanks for staying."

"I was worried," she whispered. "I couldn't leave you like that."

His fingers plucked at the top button of her blouse and slipped it free. "It felt good to know you cared. But I want to make it so you'll never have to leave me, Leia. I'm tired of being alone. I'd like to wake up every morning and find you in bed beside me, lovely and warm and tumbled from my loving."

Leia's breath caught at the intensity of his words. He slipped another button free, then another. She reached out to stop him, placing her hand on the warm, lightly furred expanse of his chest that was exposed by the V of his robe. A lightning charge of sensation bolted up her arm to lodge low in her middle.

"Ross, I'm not sure . . ." Her voice trembled, desire and caution warring within her.

He sighed deeply and rested his forehead against hers, letting his fingertips trail in erotic circles from her throat down her breastbone. "Then let me touch you, just for a little while. Let me learn you. One step at a time, Leia."

Leia gazed into his hazel eyes and knew that she could trust this sensitive, perceptive man. She slipped her hand under the drape of his robe and lifted her mouth. Ross's lips covered hers, gently at first, then with growing pressure. Her thumb found the rounded, pebbled nub of his nipple and he groaned, deepening the kiss with a fiery plunge of his tongue. His fingers peeled aside the edges of her shirt, then his mouth moved from her lips, down her throat to the beginning swells of her breasts covered by her sheer lacy bra.

She touched his hair, urging him closer. She felt the moistness of his breath through the lace, then gasped when his mouth closed over the pouty bud and sucked gently through the fabric. His hand cupped her other breast, massaging it into turgid arousal to match its twin. Leia moaned, pressing feverish kisses to his temple and nuzzling his spice-brown hair.

Ross slid his hands down her back, pulling her down on top of him as he fell back lengthways on the sofa. He recaptured her mouth, seeking and devouring as their legs tangled. Leia reached for him, miscalculated, placed her hand in the air and slid right off him and onto the floor.

"Ouch!"

"Are you okay?" Ross reached for her, his eyes still hooded with passion.

Leia rubbed her bruised posterior and suddenly began to laugh. "Is this tumbled enough for you, Ross?" she asked, giggling.

Ross gave a reluctant chuckle, and the fire in his eyes

dimmed to a glow. "That wasn't exactly what I had in mind," he admitted with a crooked grin. He swung his long bare legs to the floor and beckoned invitingly with his dark brows. "But if you'd care to continue . . . ?"

Leia picked herself up and began to button her blouse. "You tempt me; you really do."

"But?"

"But I've got to get to work, and if you're well enough for this kind of highjinks, then you're well enough to drive me home."

He gave a sigh and grimaced. "That's what I was afraid you'd say. Okay, ladybird. One step at a time. You set the pace, but it's merely a postponement of the inevitable."

Her feminine core contracted at the promise in his words, and she wondered why she hesitated. He would be a demanding, passionate lover, tender and caring. Her body screamed for fulfillment, but still she held back. When she made that decision, she had to be sure, because she knew when she gave herself to Ross in a physical union, there would be no turning back.

"I'll try to remember that," she murmured.

Ross rose and gave her a long look and a fleeting kiss. It wasn't many minutes before they were speeding toward her house. He looked dynamic and handsome in standard Navy khakis, and the cool November breeze ruffled his hair as he drove.

"I'll let you know about the arrangements for this weekend," he said when he stopped in front of her house. "You aren't going to back out on me, are you?"

She shook her head and steeled herself not to cringe at the thought of seeing the Blue Angels' performance in New Orleans. "No, I'll be there Saturday morning. I can't leave Elizabeth by herself in the shop on Friday, but I've got a girl to take my place Saturday."

"Good." He squeezed her hand.

Leia bit her lip. "Ross? Will you let Pete Neely take a look at you—just to be on the safe side? That dizziness isn't something you should mess around with." Her expression was very serious, but he laughed off her fears.

"Hey, don't worry. I'm as fit as a fiddle!"

"I just want you to be sure."

"I'll take care of it, ladybird. You just start packing. We're going to have a great time together this weekend."

Leia thought about his words while she washed up for work. She couldn't help the tiny thrill of fear that whispered its warning despite his confident assurances. One step at a time, she told herself, and sent a silent prayer heavenward for courage.

On Saturday morning Leia sat down on the bed in the plush hotel room and tried to think. It wasn't easy. The closer she got to actually seeing Ross fly, the more nervous she became. She took a deep breath and stuffed her room key into her bag.

It was early still, and her dawn drive from Pensacola to New Orleans via Interstate 10 had been easy and uneventful. She'd even managed to negotiate the dreadful New Orleans traffic. Ross had thought of everything. He'd booked her a room at the same hotel where he and the team had been staying since Thursday. That day they'd had meetings with the media, and she knew that Friday they had flown a practice show as part of the Navy recruiting effort, inviting groups from hospitals, schools, and nursing homes to attend. But Saturday and Sunday were for the public. Ross had mentioned some of his commitments for public appearances while he was in the Crescent City, and Leia knew he would be busy. She realized that he was on duty and might not have much time for her. But that wasn't the point, she reminded herself firmly. This was her chance to prove to herself that she could handle his flying. She tried not to think about Mitch or Stephen.

Leia picked up the phone and dialed the number of Ross's room.

"Leia, are you here already?" Ross's husky voice sounded delighted. "I just got out of the shower. I'm on the floor above you. Come on up. Room 721."

A quick trip in an elevator later Leia stood in the heavily carpeted hall, hesitating. She straightened her green and gold geometric sweater and matching skirt and shot a surreptitious glance down the empty hall. She knocked quietly.

Ross flung open the door, a boyish grin splitting his face. He wore the Blue Angels Nomex flight suit, and his hair was damp and freshly combed. Leia couldn't help the silly smile that curved her lips. He reached out and nearly jerked her into the room, slamming the door behind her and gathering her close in his powerful embrace.

"Why do I have such a clandestine and sinful feeling about coming to a man's room?" Leia asked, her expression teasing.

"I don't know," Ross murmured. "But we might as well give you something to really feel guilty about."

He proceeded to kiss her passionately. When he at last lifted his head, Leia's knees felt like jelly and she was sighing with pleasure.

"Lord, I've missed you," Ross said. He pulled back and studied her narrowly. "You doing okay?"

"Better, now."

"Not too nervous?"

She shook her head. "I won't freak out on you, I promise."

"Remember what I told you."

She ticked the numbers off on her fingers. "One, you're

the best pilot in the whole damn Navy. Two, you know the routines inside out and backward and could fly them in your sleep. Three, you know your aircraft. Four, you trust your teammates completely. Five . . . five?" She gave him a questioning look.

"Five," he said softly, catching her shoulders and staring down into her eyes. "Five, I love you, Leia Conner McKenzie, and I will always come home to you."

"Five," she echoed, touched to her very center by the sincerity of his words. She put her arms around his neck and pressed against him. "Hold me, Ross, just for a moment."

"Always glad to oblige a lady." He pressed his face against her neck and inhaled the fresh floral odor of her perfume. Lord, she was going to do it! His heart leapt for joy. This was it! She would come to terms with his way of life today. He had no doubts about her. He knew her strengths, knew the fine tensile steel in her backbone. He wanted her so badly, in all ways. He was hungry for the physical intimacy, but it was more than that. For the first time in his adult life, he knew what it was to care about someone else more than himself. And Leia's happiness was his happiness. The future stretched before him like a golden road map, filled with magical choices and exciting possibilities. Ross's heart swelled with love and hope. He dropped a little kiss on her temple.

"I'm starving. How about some breakfast?"

"You're always hungry," she said.

He could hear the smile in her voice. "Your choice. What do you want?"

"Beignets and café au lait," she answered promptly.

He groaned. "Hardly what a growing boy like myself needs." He relented at the disappointed look on her face. "All right. First we go downstairs for real food, then I'll take you to Jackson Square for beignets. Deal?"

"Deal!"

Leia watched Ross polish off a hearty breakfast of bacon and eggs, coffee, toast, and grits, then they caught a taxi to the French Quarter. At Café du Monde on the edge of Jackson Square, Ross drank a second cup of dark Louisiana coffee while Leia feasted on a plate of the fried bread squares dusted with powdered sugar that are the Creole doughnut. It was still early, too early to investigate the shops in the renovated Jax Brewery building across the square, but they strolled around the cool shaded pavilions of the Cabildo and St. Louis Cathedral. They inspected the statue of Andrew Jackson on his rearing horse in the center of the grassy square, and Leia teased Ross about his call sign, Hickory, saying that Jackson's stern profile matched Ross's. They laughed together, and the coo of pigeons was a soft counterpoint. At last Ross said they had to get back to the hotel so he could rejoin the team and leave for the New Orleans naval air station.

"I hate to leave you on your own like this," Ross said as they crossed the crowded lobby.

"I understand perfectly. Don't worry. You've got other things you need to concentrate on."

"You've got that press pass, haven't you? And you know to meet Lieutenant Jarvis at the public affairs office. He'll see that you get a seat in the VIP bleachers."

"I'll be all right," she assured him.

"Say, mister! Can I have your autograph?" An awestruck kid of about twelve pushed a brochure and pen at Ross.

"Sure, son. Here you go. You coming out to see the air show today?"

"I sure am! Golly, thanks!"

"I'll wave to you," Ross said, winking. He hustled Leia toward the elevator.

"Are you going to miss all this when it's over?" Leia asked

when the elevator doors slid shut. "The publicity and the hero worship?"

"In a way. It's been great being a member of the Blues. It's like an exclusive fraternity. I'll miss it, but it's time to graduate. I don't have any doubts that I'll find some new challenges after I leave." He hooked his arm around her waist and grinned down at her, full of confidence and vigor.

Leia smiled back, feeling some of her doubts and tension leave her. How could anything go wrong? Ross knew what he was doing. He had been doing it successfully for nearly two years, not to mention all the other planes he'd flown during his years in the Navy. Why hadn't she realized that before?

"I'll meet you back here after we debrief, okay?" Ross asked.

"Fine. I'll be waiting."

A feeling of calm stole over her. Everything was going to be all right. Soon, after she had proved herself, she would be able to tell this wonderful, marvelous man just what he'd come to mean to her.

Leia wiped the trickle of perspiration running down her neck and gazed anxiously across the flight line at Naval Air Station New Orleans. The bright November sun was a white glare on the tarmac and the sky was a dazzling, cloudless blue. The temperature rose steadily into the balmy seventies. The crowd of over a hundred thousand rumbled around her like a muted roar of thunder.

She had been escorted with great efficiency by Lieutenant Jarvis along with other special visitors through the standing-room-only throng to the cordoned-off section of VIP bleachers. Presenting her pass to the white-uniformed MPs allowed her entrance into a striped tent pavilion decorated with hanging baskets of ferns protecting ranks of folding chairs. Leia chose a seat in the stands fronting the pavilion. She was surrounded by high-ranking military brass and their families, and political bigwigs from the city of New Orleans. She shifted on the hard metal bench and wrinkled her nose at the acrid odor of diesel exhaust. Lieutenant Jarvis, a fresh-faced young officer, chatted amiably about the upcoming program.

Leia shaded her eyes against the glare and scanned the runway for Ross. There had been other performances by the Army's Silver Eagles helicopter team and the Golden Knights parachute team as well as some barnstormers and a glider that had suitably awed and amazed the spectators. But now it was time for the main event—the Blue Angels.

The six blue-and-gold Hornets sat side by side in a silent row directly in front of the VIP bleachers, waiting for their turn in the air. Leia gripped the edges of the metal seat and tried to bolster her faltering courage. She would not let Ross down—or herself. She wouldn't!

The deep bass voice of Blue Angel number seven, Lieutenant Tom Young, the team narrator, boomed over the loudspeakers in an introduction. The ground crew scurried into position. Leia sat up straight. Six pilots in Blue Angel gold and blue marched down the flight line, dropping off at each plane as the narrator introduced each officer. She counted them—one, two, three—Ross!

She strained forward, concentrating on Ross, taking in the military bearing and precision of his movements, the snappy salute to his ground crew. Her focus narrowed until he was all she saw, the surrounding crowd and even Lieutenant Jarvis fading into the nether reaches of her consciousness. Then he and the other team members scaled the narrow ladders simultaneously to disappear into the planes' cockpits. Gold helmets in place, six canopies swung down,

113

and the ear-battering whine of six F/A-18 Hornets drowned out all further thought.

One by one the Hornets taxied forward, turned, and followed the Boss in Blue Angel Number One single-file down the flight line. The narrator pointed out that even taxiing, they kept "minimum separation," and Leia chewed her lip, for there seemed only a hand's breadth between each plane. Lieutenant Young kept up a running commentary while the planes took position at the far end of the runway. A second later there was a burst of flash and thunder as four jets, all heat and smoke, raced down the runway.

Leia gasped, almost feeling the thrust of those powerful engines against her own body. The earth fell away for Leia as she watched the blue-and-gold planes vault into space, slipping into the familiar diamond formation. Four separate machines, merely thirty-six inches apart at wingtip and canopy, moved as if they were a single entity.

With another roar and burst of smoke, the two solo pilots took off behind their compatriots. The crowd applauded and cheered, but Leia followed the tiny specks of a diamond in the sky until they were lost somewhere in the blue reaches of the horizon. Within seconds they reappeared, performing to the measured cadences of number seven over the loudspeakers.

For the next few minutes that diamond kept trading places with the two solo planes, executing an aerial ballet of finesse and power, graceful rolls and loops alternating with gut-wrenching near-misses. The crowd ohhed and ahhed, shrieked in terror and cheered wildly. Leia sat silently, her mind firmly fixed on the left-wing position, her concentration on one man, one plane, as if any wavering of her attention might entice disaster. She was so firmly focused on the plane with the big gold number 3 emblazoned on its tail, she could almost see the cockpit, see Ross's big hand on the stick, see the tumble and twirl of earth and sky through the canopy.

The diamond screamed across the flight line once again, noses lifting, then climbed into the vertical, standing the jets on their tails for a long moment. This was the critical period of slowest velocity and highest power as they formed the diamond loop.

Near the top of the curve the number-three jet suddenly lagged behind, then fell off to the left. There was a delayed vibration in the air, more concussion than sound.

Leia leapt to her feet, her hands pressed against her white lips, her heart stopped in her breast. "Oh, no!" she whispered, transfixed.

The number-three jet cleared the formation, peeling off in a perpendicular line away from the runway, skimming over the ground to disappear below the far-distant treetops toward the glint of the Mississippi River. The three remaining members of the diamond completed the loop and tore off along the flight line. The sky was empty, the crowd unnaturally silent.

Number seven's voice echoed over the loudspeakers. "Ladies and gentlemen, we have a momentary delay in today's show. Lieutenant Commander Walker reports a maintenance difficulty."

Maintenance difficulty? What the hell did *that* mean? Leia pressed a white-knuckled fist against her mouth. Terror was an icy ball in her chest. Frantically she scanned the empty sky.

Where was Ross?

CHAPTER SEVEN

"Where is he?" Leia's fingers dug into Lieutenant Jarvis's arm in a physical demand for an answer. "Is—is he down?"

"No, ma'am. At least, there's no smoke. He must have lost an engine." He pointed in a wide arc toward the horizon. "He'll have to circle around to get downwind to land."

Frantically Leia scanned the green treetops, willing Ross's plane to reappear. The crowd murmured around her as if unaware of the danger.

Don't they know? Don't they understand? her brain screamed. Did only she and Lieutenant Jarvis realize that there was something seriously wrong?

There was a scurrying of ground crew at the far end of the runway, the flash of personnel and equipment moving swiftly, purposefully. Leia's eyes widened at the fleet of emergency equipment moving into place. She shuddered and tore her gaze away, searching the empty skies, her lips moving in silent, wordless prayer.

"There he is." Lieutenant Jarvis's voice was matter-of-fact.

"Oh, God."

The Hornet loomed low over the trees, wavered in the changeable air currents, and limped toward the runway.

Oh, no. Oh, no. Oh, no! Leia's mind shrieked. *Don't crash! Don't die, Ross, don't die!*

116

The plane roared toward the earth, eased lower, touched down with a faint bounce, then flashed past in a scream of heat and smoking tires. He was down!

Leia's knees buckled in reaction. She sat down hard, her breathing ragged. Ross was safe! She felt light-headed, giddy.

Beside her, Lieutenant Jarvis grunted in satisfaction. "There he goes."

She craned her neck to watch Ross's progress. The number-three plane taxied around, halted. Before she could smile her relief, Ross was down the ladder and running toward another waiting plane that was warming up on the runway.

Leia struggled to her feet, disbelief written on her white face. "What? He's not going up again?"

Lieutenant Jarvis shrugged. "Sure. He'll take the replacement jet."

The narrator resumed his commentary at that moment, explaining that Lieutenant Commander Walker would be able to complete the show using the blue-and-gold replacement aircraft. The crowd applauded, and the single jet roared down the runway and was airborne. The entire procedure had taken about four minutes.

Something in Leia snapped. A tiny, frantic whimper escaped her. She clapped a hand over her mouth, certain the next sound from her would be insane, hysterical laughter. How could he do this to her? Scare her to death, then relieve her fears, only to start the terrifying vicious cycle again! It was an up-and-down ride on a whirling carousel. Was that the price she must pay for loving Ross Walker?

"Here they come," Lieutenant Jarvis announced. "Looks like they'll attempt the diamond loop again."

Leia couldn't watch. She scrambled down from the

bleachers, her movements jerky, clutching her purse like a lifeline.

"Ma'am? Are you okay?" Lieutenant Jarvis called after her. "What about . . . ?"

She raised her hand in a half-hearted wave and plunged through the crowd, passing the uniformed MPs, almost running across the concrete airstrip, weaving her way past the different aircraft on display. She winced at the roar of jet engines passing behind her on the flight line, the applause of the crowd grating on her overstretched nerves. It was a long walk to her car, and she didn't even realize until she reached it that she was crying.

Leia sat in a chair in the lamp-lit hotel room and stared sightlessly out the window at the New Orleans skyline. The great white humpbacked bowl of the Superdome rose like a beached whale across the street. Streetlights and car headlights and neon signs lit up the night like a Christmas tree. Down on Bourbon Street the strip joints and oyster bars and jazz quartets would just be cranking up for the usual Saturday night party, Creole-style. And none of it held any interest for Leia.

A thunderous pounding rattled the door. Leia flew on stocking feet to fling it open, to fill her eyes with Ross—hale and whole and utterly beloved. She reached for him and he scooped her up, her arms locked about his neck, his arms folded around her waist. He held her effortlessly, her feet dangling above the floor. He walked them into the room, her face buried against his neck, and kicked the door shut.

"I was afraid you'd gone," he said thickly.

"No." The word was a soft sob.

Ross tried to look at her, his heart twisting in knots. "Are you crying? Don't cry, ladybird."

She kept her face buried against his shoulder, rubbing her

cheek on the blue Nomex fabric of his fireproof flight suit, inhaling the musky male odor of sweat and shaving cream and tanned skin. "I wasn't brave," she choked out. "When I saw—and then you—" A ragged sob tore through her words.

"I had a bird strike," Ross said. "It took out an engine, but I was never in any real danger."

She leaned away from him, and he let her slide down his body until her toes touched the carpet. "Don't lie to me, Ross," she said, her voice soft and fierce. "Don't ever lie to me!"

His jaw tightened, and he knew this lady had too much savvy to accept the easy assurances. "All right. It was hairy there for a moment. I was pushing the outside of the safety envelope. But I had it under control the whole time."

"This time." The low timbre of her voice resonated with fear and a hint of bitterness.

Ross cupped her face in his hands, and his thumbs smoothed the moisture from her cheeks. "It's part of my job to know what to do in an emergency. Despite every safety precaution, sometimes things happen. Today wasn't the first time, and it won't be the last. The point is, I know what to do."

"But I don't. I let you down. I ran away again." Her lower lip trembled.

"Don't, honey," he soothed her huskily. "You survived a worst-case scenario the best you could. I think it took a lot of courage. And you're still here. That must mean something."

"It means I love you so much I can't bear the thought of losing you."

"Leia!" Ross's heart did a series of supersonic flip-flops and his fingers trembled against her skin. "Do you mean it?"

"More than anything." Her eyes were luminous blue-green pools, and her voice caught with fervent emotion. She didn't know exactly when it had become clear to her. All that mattered now was that he know. "I love you. I need you close to me. Hold me, Ross."

He gathered her close, burying his nose in her fragrant red-gold curls. His heart wanted to burst out of his chest. His dream had become reality and oh, it was sweet to savor the triumph. "Oh, God, Leia. Say it again."

"I love you."

He captured her whisper with his mouth, kissing her tenderly, trying to make her feel his love, his elation, his humility. Her lips were salty-sweet. He silently vowed never to cause her anguish, to do everything in his power to make her happy, forever and always.

Leia's thoughts reeled under the sensual caress of Ross's mouth, yet it wasn't enough, not after his brush with death. Was happiness always this bittersweet? She wanted to feel the flame of life burning strong within his lean frame, to discover for herself the depths of his passion, to deny danger and mortality with the age-old renewal of life. Her lips parted and her tongue flicked out, limning the seam of his mouth, inviting him, begging him.

Ross groaned and slanted his mouth across hers. He tasted her, traced the moist cavern of her mouth, then pulled back, opening for her dainty exploration. He bit gently at her tongue, then sucked her into his mouth and heard her whimper of desire.

He felt her growing response, sensed her need, that matched the burning fire in his loins. His hand slipped to the valley of her spine, the soft curve of her hip, pulling her closer into the cradle of his thighs. Her pelvis moved against his hardness with answering pressure and urgency. He raised his head at last and they both gasped for breath.

Closing his eyes, he let his mouth rest against her temple.

He forced himself to ask the question that haunted him. "Leia? Are you sure?"

"I'm sure of everything except how to get this damned flight suit off!"

Ross let the laughter rumble deep in his chest, the tension of the day's events replaced by soaring joy. He cupped her face and grinned down at her, his senses igniting at the smoky look in her hooded eyes, the little teasing smile on her pink lips. "I'll show you," he said.

Eager fingers found zippers and buttons, tugging clothing away and sending it sailing in all directions to float unheeded to the floor. A yellow ascot fell atop a silky slip. Her sweater was bundled up with his blue suit and made a colorful heap in the chair. Underwear disappeared with a shimmy and toss.

"Lord-a-mercy, ma'am," Ross breathed, taking in the delicate, porcelain perfection of her exquisite form. His eyes flamed golden and his breathing became ragged. He trailed a trembling finger down over the crest of one ripe, peach-hued breast, making Leia gasp. "You are just about the prettiest thing I ever did see!"

Leia in turn gazed at Ross's magnificent male physique, intrigued by the ripple and play of tightly corded muscles lightly dusted with soft curling hair. She reached for him, sliding her fingers into the soft pelt, following the whorls across his chest, testing the hard resiliency and warmth of his flesh. Ross gave her free rein to go where she would but kept his hand cupped possessively around her breast. His lids lowered and his face was etched with pleasure. Leia's fingers hesitated on a strange welt running across his shoulder.

"Ross? What is this?"

He looked down at his shoulder, a bit amazed. "Harness

must have done it. I pulled some extra g's coming out of that loop."

Leia suppressed a shudder, then slowly, slowly let her lips trace the red outline of the welt. Ross shuddered, but for another reason entirely, and his arms closed about her, pulling her tight against him so that they were skin to skin, heart to heart.

"Oh, ladybird, it's going to be so good for us." His voice was husky. He picked her up, her head resting against his shoulder.

"I know." In spite of her building excitement, there was a strange peace in Leia's soul, a fatalistic acceptance of a destiny that linked her life and Ross's. It was hard, but at this moment it was also very right.

Ross placed her on the bed as though she were a fragile and infinitely precious burden. With his mouth and his hands he cherished her, showing her with his caresses the countless ways they could pleasure each other. He stroked her satin thighs, his large hands gentle yet forceful where she needed to feel his power. His lips nuzzled at the V in her collarbone, moved lower and swept in tantalizing circles around the swollen orbs of her breasts until she was gasping with delight and frustration. His mouth closed over a rosy pebbled peak and she cried out, urging him closer with her hands at the base of his strong neck and running her fingers through his short brown hair.

She was on fire with a burning need for him that melted her feminine center. But she couldn't just take from him, not when her heart was full to overflowing. It was important that she give as well. She shivered uncontrollably as he moved his lips to her other nipple. Her hand rested against the side of his jaw, feeling the faint rasp of beard and the erotic movement of his cheek as he suckled. With a moan of pleasure she tugged him upward, meeting his lips in a fiery kiss. Squirming against him, she pushed gently on his shoulder, reversing their positions.

Now it was her turn to torment him, to bring him to a fevered pitch with the delightful little things her hands could do. She felt his start of surprise and smiled against his lips.

"Did you think you were going to have all the fun?" she murmured, dropping kisses down his chin, across his chest, teasing at the bronze coins of his nipples.

Leia's hands slid down his taut abdomen, following the tapering line of hair. Boldly she stroked the heated, throbbing proof of his passion.

"You're asking for trouble, ma'am," he said with a growl from low in his throat.

She laughed softly. "I think I've found it. And don't 'ma'am' me, flyboy!"

"Yes, ma'am. No, ma'am!" She punished his insubordination by multiplying her efforts. He gasped and groaned. "Christ, Leia!"

In an instant she found herself flat on her back again, Ross looming over her, his features taut with need. He took her mouth again, and she answered him fully, clutching feverishly at his broad shoulders and arching against him in sensual invitation.

"Ross!" His name was her plea for him to begin what they both so desperately wanted.

"Now?"

"Yes!"

He position himself between her thighs and with supreme control eased forward, sinking deep within her, filling her. They rocked together, savoring the first moment of being one, holding tight to each other for a long silver eternity. With one accord they began to move, finding a rhythm that brought forth tiny cries of ecstasy from Leia's throat.

She was flying, soaring on a plane so far above anything she had ever experienced that she thought she must surely touch the stars. Locked in his arms, Leia knew the fire and magic of Ross's love. An exquisite tension was built within her until she was completely outside herself, reaching, stretching. Her release came out of the blue, surprising her with its power, a soul-wrenching explosion of pleasure that sent her spinning. She arched forward with Ross's name on her lips, heard his massive groan as he plunged after her into fulfillment.

They lay for a long time, too spent to move, their bodies slick with moisture. At last Ross eased away, kissing her tenderly and pulling her into the curve of his shoulder.

"For a little bit of a ladybird, you are one dynamite woman," he said, grinning up at the ceiling.

Leia settled more comfortably against him, her cheek on his chest. She could hear the still-erratic patter of his heart beneath her ear. "I've never felt so special—so loved—in all my life," she whispered.

"Well, get used to it. Now that I've got you I'm not letting go."

"I hear you." She sighed contentedly and began tracing little circles on his chest with her fingertip. His stomach rumbled, and she laughed. "Hungry as usual, huh, Ross?"

"Uh-huh. You want to go out for some New Orleans seafood?"

Leia raised herself and propped her elbow against his chest. Her smile was a mixture of imp and seductress. "What would you do if I said I'd rather have room service?"

Ross laughed and pulled her close, feeling the first stirring of desire returning. "Ladybird, I'd count my lucky stars!"

Leia didn't get to see any of the New Orleans nightlife. She and Ross made their own entertainment throughout the night.

The morning sky held the last wisps of river fog when Leia eased from the bed they'd shared. Ross lay sprawled on his back, deeply asleep, his flesh a dark contrast to the rumpled white sheets. Leia smiled at the boyish cast of his features relaxed in slumber. Quietly she picked up their scattered clothing. Her limbs felt strangely weak and lethargic, every tension gone, soothed under the power of Ross's lovemaking. But in the clear light of day, doubts began to sneak back into her mind. She stole another look at Ross and stifled a sigh. Taking her overnight bag, she headed toward the bathroom.

When she returned, showered and dressed in slacks and a cotton sweater, Ross was stirring. He opened a bleary eye and then stretched, a bone-popping extension that made him shiver from his fingertips to his toes. He gave a wide yawn and rubbed his hand back and forth through his hair. His smile was sleepy and warmly sensual.

"Morning."

"Hi, sleepyhead." Leia smiled back almost shyly, a rosy blush coloring her cheeks at the memory of their lusty abandon. She finished stuffing her things into her bag, then zipped and locked it.

"Come over here, woman, so I can say good morning properly," he ordered, plumping up the pillows and settling back comfortably. The sheet was draped modestly across his lap, but he was big and virile and oh, so attractive!

Leia couldn't resist the invitation. She sat down beside him on the edge of the bed. "Is saying good morning as enjoyable as saying good night?" she asked.

Ross chuckled and reached for her. "We'll find out."

Leia was faintly dizzy when he ended the kiss.

"Well? What do you think?" he asked with a grin.

"I think that I'm in big trouble," she said with a sigh.

"Maybe you need to conduct more research on the question. I'll be happy to volunteer." His hand massaged her shoulder, then swept down to cup her breast through the thick sweater. He frowned. "You're dressed already."

Leia pulled back and glanced away. "Yes. I—I've got to get home."

The notch between Ross's brows deepened. "You aren't staying for the show this afternoon?"

Her eyes were wide and pleading for his understanding. "I can't. Please don't ask me."

His disappointment was apparent, and he started to say something, then stopped. His jaw tightened. "All right. If everything goes okay, we'll probably fly home after the show and debrief there. I'll call you as soon as I'm done. Is that okay?" His tone was a bit belligerent.

"Yes, of course," she hastened to say. "It's just that . . ."

"Regrets, Leia? Second thoughts?" His voice was silky.

"No, not that."

"Then what?" He caught her shoulders and forced her to face him. "Dammit! I love you, Leia! I want to marry you! Why do you doubt me? Isn't it enough for you?"

"I'm not sure," she whispered, licking dry lips.

"Not sure! Even after last night?" he demanded harshly. "Didn't it mean anything to you?"

"Ross, please! I'm trying very hard to—to come to terms with what it will mean. I'm not saying no. I need a little time, that's all. Everything's happened so fast!"

"Time is something we're running out of, ladybird."

"I do love you, Ross." Her voice was low. "You've got to believe that."

Ross heaved a sigh and pulled her against his chest. His heart ached for the torment in her words. "I believe you."

"I have to convince myself that what I'm feeling isn't just all in my mind. I need you, Ross. But I need to know that I

126

can handle this kind of commitment without letting you down. I haven't got a very good track record."

He looked down into her eyes, and his voice was thick with sudden emotion. "As long as you're with me, you could never let me down."

Her laugh was shaky. "You have more confidence than I do."

"I've got enough for two."

His mouth covered hers, sealing his promise. Somehow he had to make her trust herself, to see that out of their love would come the strength she needed. If what she needed now was for him to back off from pressuring her, then that was what she'd get from him. But now that he knew exactly what he'd be missing if he lost her, it was hard—damn hard.

Leia entered her empty house later that afternoon after driving back from New Orleans. She'd shared breakfast with Ross, relieved that he didn't seem angry with her any longer. She'd left after that, pointing out that he had to get ready for his afternoon performance by catching up on his sleep. He couldn't argue about that!

The long ride had given her plenty of time to think—too much, really. She was jumpy and anxious about her relationship with Ross. She knew that she couldn't keep putting him off indefinitely. He was a man of action, and to try to keep him on hold would be an exercise in futility. But she just didn't know if she could live the life he wanted.

She threw down her overnight bag and purse and made a restless tour around the silent house. Not a thing out of place to indicate anyone really *lived* here, she thought glumly.

Marrying Ross would entail giving up the things she had worked for. She would have to find someone else to take over The Gingerbread House with Elizabeth, and give up the stability of having a permanent home. She could always go back to nursing to see her through the lonely months when Ross would be on sea duty, but none of these things was the real problem. It all boiled down to one thing: did she have the courage to love him and to let him go each morning knowing that he might not return to her?

Her feet took her to the bookshelf where Mitch and Stephen stared from their picture frames with silent, accusing eyes. The walls suddenly seemed to be closing in on her. She couldn't stand being alone, even in her own home where she had always felt so secure. She grabbed her keys and windbreaker and headed for the car, intent on escape.

Leia drove aimlessly for a while. She was tempted to visit Elizabeth but then decided against it. Elizabeth had always been able to read her too well, and Leia did not yet feel that she was at a point that she could discuss her feelings with anyone. She pulled through the drive-in window of a fast food restaurant, ate a hamburger she didn't even taste, and continued to drive. Instinctively she skirted the edge of the bay, passed The Gingerbread House, and headed for the beach.

On the western point of Santa Rosa Island lay the entrance to the Gulf Islands National Seashore preserve, a narrow strip of primitive barrier island that was a haven for wildlife. Leia drove through the gates, leaving the jumble of beach-side condominiums and tourist development behind. During the summer the park's campgrounds were usually packed, but on this blustery November day there was little activity. Leia drove until she passed the massive brick fortress that was the remains of Fort Pickens. She parked on the frontage road that curved around the tip of the island near the public fishing pier. A few stalwart fishermen dipped their lines into the bayside waters.

Leia climbed the concrete steps over the sea wall and

walked down onto the white, powdery sand. Jamming her hands into the pockets of her windbreaker, she lifted her face to the salty wind. The raucous call of a trio of gulls punctuated the crash and dash of the surf.

She walked for a long time, stopping occasionally to pick up a bit of seashell, the broken edge of a sand dollar. The sun filtered through high white clouds, touching the water in bands of emerald green, turquoise, and, where the floor of the Gulf dropped off, a deep dark blue. After a while she turned and retraced her steps, coming again to the point of the island where the sea and the bay met in a clash of surf and current. She climbed up on the sea wall and gazed across the narrow neck of the bay at the chunky outlines of the buildings and hangars of Naval Air Station Pensacola. She could just make out the dark shape of the aircraft carrier *Lexington* at dock.

She sat down to wait.

The sun was a ball diving into the water directly in front of her when Leia first heard the faint roar of distant thunder. She shaded her eyes, searching the sky. She saw it at last, contrasted against the pink-tinted clouds.

A sextet of gold-and-blue Hornets, homing slowly toward Sherman Field, formed a flying triangle, the "delta" formation of the Blue Angels. Leia stood, dusting the grains of damp sand from her pants. Her eyes searched out the left wing aircraft and stayed on it as the delta made a pass over the naval air station. In a long graceful turn it made a full circle out over the Gulf and back, then dipped below the trees on the distant shore and disappeared.

Leia let out the breath she'd been holding. There was undeniable beauty in flight: she had to acknowledge it, and maybe, in that instant, she began to understand what held Ross to his chosen calling.

Ross. He'd be phoning soon. She'd better start for home. When she arrived she went directly to the bookshelf and carefully, tenderly took down Mitch's photograph and put it away for good.

CHAPTER EIGHT

Leia stirred the pot of shrimp gumbo and glanced again at the clock. Only ten minutes had passed since the last time she had looked. She set down the spoon and wiped her hands, then paused to adjust the angle of a soup spoon at the table set for two. Satisfied, she crossed to the sink and gazed out into the darkness, her teeth worrying her bottom lip.

Where was Ross? Why hadn't he called? She'd dialed his number, but it only rang unanswered in her ear. Had something happened to delay him at the base? He could still call her, couldn't he?

She unconsciously smoothed her hair and tugged at the sleeves of her appliquéd sweatshirt. She swallowed harshly and forced herself to face the fear that had been nagging at her, the anxiety she'd tried to deny by cooking a meal, showering, and taking an inordinate amount of time over the table setting while she waited for him. Maybe . . . maybe he was having second thoughts himself. Maybe he regretted making love to her. Maybe, on reflection, he had decided that she was more trouble than she was worth.

Leia shook her head in an effort to banish such thoughts. No, Ross was a man of the highest integrity. His word was his bond. He wouldn't say he loved her if he didn't mean it. Her doubts were a reflection of her own guilt, a guilt an-

131

chored in the fear and hatred she felt for his way of life. She didn't want to come between him and his flying career, knowing that if he had to make a choice, the only result would be a resentment that could destroy their love. And when it came down to it, she wasn't completely certain what his choice would be. Yet she didn't know if they could mesh their lives despite the deep, growing emotional ties that bound them. It was a quandary she couldn't resolve. All she knew was that she needed Ross. When she was with him, anything seemed possible.

The phone rang, shattering her concentration, and she pounced on it. "Hello?"

"Leia, this is Ross."

She knew immediately from the leaden tone of his voice that something was wrong. "What's the matter? Where are you?"

"I'm at Pam's. Haven't you heard?"

"Heard what?" He was with Pamela Anderson? Merely a block over? But he'd promised to come here! A throbbing lump of jealousy and hurt swelled in her chest.

"You mean you don't know? Turn on your television." He was impatient, sharp. "There's been a skirmish in the Gulf of Sidra. There's a chance Webb's been shot down."

"Oh, no." His flat, brutal revelation pierced her, shocked her to the core. Leia felt deeply ashamed of her unworthy emotions of the moment before. "How's Pamela?"

"As well as can be expected. I'm trying to get through to the squadron duty office at Oceana now." His voice dropped. "I'm sorry, ladybird. I'd give anything to be with you, but Pamela needs me."

Leia swallowed and said the hardest words in her life. "I understand. He's your best friend. Of course you have to be there for Pam. Tell me how to help." She could hear his ragged breath.

"You just did."

"You'll let me know just as soon as you hear anything?"

"Of course."

"I love you, Ross."

He groaned. "Remind me to kiss you the next time I see you."

She laughed softly. "Count on it, flyboy."

Leia hung up the phone, then walked over to the television and flipped it on. She frowned at the granite-faced news commentator informing her that this was a special bulletin. The crisis in the Mediterranean involved aircraft scrambled from the carrier *Nimitz* to intercept unidentified hostile fighters. It was clear there was not much information available, although speculation ran rampant. More than one nation in the Mideast hated the United States. That was all Leia could learn although she continued to check the other stations for the rest of the evening.

There was nothing new Monday, either, even though Elizabeth kept her small portable radio turned on at The Gingerbread House all day.

"You'd think they'd be able to tell us more by now!" Elizabeth complained in disgust toward the end of the day.

"It's frustrating, but just think how the families must feel," Leia agreed.

"It's more than frustrating, it's downright un-American! The public has a right to know what's going on." Elizabeth pushed back the wisps of graying hair that had fallen out of her bun with an absentminded swipe. "Oh, horsefeathers! I can't make these figures come out right. See if you can."

Leia joined her godmother at the cash register and began to readd the day's receipts, her slim fingers flying over the calculator buttons. Elizabeth peered over her half-glasses and studied Leia's expression closely.

"In all the hubbub I forgot to ask," she said casually. "Did you enjoy the air show this weekend?"

Leia's fingers hesitated on the buttons. "No," she said shortly. She punched in a few more numbers, hit the total key, and pulled the tape out of the machine. "There, that's okay now."

"Wait a minute! What do you mean, no?"

Leia licked her lips. "I mean it scared me to death. Ross sucked a bird into an engine, knocking it out. He had to come down fast. It was . . ." She shook her head, at a loss to describe her terror. "And now this thing with Webb Anderson maybe going down in the Mediterranean. I don't know what to do or how I feel."

"If you can't deal with it," Elizabeth said slowly, "maybe you shouldn't see Ross again."

"It's too late for that. I—I'm in love with him."

"That's wonderful!" Elizabeth frowned. "Or is it? Honey, I hope you know what you're doing."

Leia gave a shaky laugh. "No, I'm just muddling through as usual. He wants to get married."

"Well, at least his intentions are honorable," Elizabeth said with a chuckle.

"Yes, they are. He's strong, and honorable, and brave, and wonderful, and so damn near perfect that sometimes I almost wish I could find something wrong with him! Then at least I would have a reason for sending him out of my life!" Her voice caught.

"Is that what you intend to do?" Elizabeth asked gently.

"No. I can't." Leia wiped at the damp corner of her eye and smiled crookedly. "I'm a coward all the way around. I'm afraid to say yes and afraid to let him go. So I'm driving us both crazy!" She took a deep breath and straightened her shoulders. "But what I intend to do tonight is take that pot of gumbo I cooked over to Pamela's and help if I can. Let's

134

see. Do you think Biddie would like one of these Santa Bears?"

Elizabeth quietly agreed that Biddie would and thought to herself that her goddaughter was braver than she knew.

Leia had every intention of merely dropping off the food that evening, but when she saw the dark circles under Pamela's eyes, she found herself bustling into the little blue house and issuing orders like an admiral.

"No, don't bother to protest, Pamela," Leia said. "You'll all feel better with a hot meal in you and I've got it right here. Gumbo, rice, and salad all ready. Let me heat it up while you tell me the news."

"There isn't any," Pamela said tiredly. She sat heavily in a chair at the kitchen table. She forced a weak smile. "But isn't no news good news?"

"That's what they say."

Leia adjusted the heat under her pots. The shrill, noisy buffoonery of a television cartoon show drifted in from the living room. Pamela grimaced.

"I don't know how Ross can sleep through all that noise. And Biddie has been so hyper! At least the cartoons have her interest for the moment."

"Ross is asleep?"

"On the couch. He spent most of last night and today on the phone trying to get word, but either they don't know anything or they aren't saying. The Navy's on alert and nothing's getting in or out." Pamela's lower lip trembled and she clamped her teeth down tight over it.

Leia sat down next to Pamela and squeezed her hand reassuringly. "I'm sure everything will work out."

"Oh, Webb's all right. I know it. It's just this waiting!"

"I know, but try to relax. The tension isn't good for you or the baby." Leia asked several pointed questions about Pamela's condition and felt better at the answers she gave.

"You might try your Lamaze relaxation exercises, too. And while Ross is around, make him help you practice your breathing techniques."

"I had a feeling there was more than supper cooking in here," Ross said.

He stood in the doorway, stretching like a grizzly bear coming out of hibernation. For the first time in Leia's memory he was less than immaculately groomed. There was a dark shadow of beard stubble on his cheeks, his shirt was wrinkled, and his hair was mussed. Leia's heart tripped over at the sight of him.

"I get worried when I see the two of you with your pretty heads together," Ross said in his drawl.

His lazy words belied the tap dance his heart was doing in his chest at the sight of Leia. Lord, she was beautiful! Soft and pretty in a frilly blouse and slacks, and so damned lovely he wanted to gobble her up and use her warmth and loveliness to lose himself, to forget everything but her. But he couldn't do that yet. There was Webb to worry about. Webb who counted on Ross to look after his family in just such a circumstance as this. Personal feelings had to be put aside for now. But God! He was glad she was here!

He ambled up beside her and dropped a lingering kiss on Leia's upturned mouth. His large, sleep-warm hand rested possessively at the nape of her neck. "Hello, ladybird."

"Hi," she breathed, her bones jelly.

"Ladybird?" Pamela queried.

Ross's mobile mouth quirked upward. "Leia's call sign. Mmm, what smells so good?"

Leia laughed. "You could be a gentleman and say it's my perfume, but I'm sure you'd be more interested in the gumbo on the stove." She shot a humorous glance at Pamela. "When he asks what's cooking, he really means it!"

"Don't I know it. That man can eat me out of house and

home. He's almost as bad as Webb." Pamela's smile faded and she blinked rapidly to force back incipient tears. She took a deep breath and continued valiantly. "You'll practice the Lamaze exercises with me, won't you, Ross?"

"They'll be better for her than a tranquilizer," Leia said quietly.

"Sure, Pam. Anytime you say." Ross's voice was gruff. He cleared his throat and turned to the stove, lifting lids on the bubbling pots. "This looks pretty good, Pam. When did you have time to make it?"

"Leia brought it."

"No!" Mock-disbelief lifted his dark brows, and his eyes sparkled with mischief.

"I can cook," Leia protested.

"We'll see," he said teasingly.

Leia rose from her chair, waving a large spoon. She tried to keep up the light banter for Pamela's sake by threatening Ross with mayhem if he continued to insult her gumbo.

"Mommy, there's no more cartoons!" Biddie wailed loudly, appearing suddenly from the living room and flinging herself on her mother's overfull lap.

"Bridget, please. I can't hold you that way," Pamela said. "Sit here in the chair beside me."

"No!" Biddie's face puckered up and her lower lip took on a sulky line.

Leia and Ross glanced at each other, understanding full well that Biddie's behavior was a reflection of the tension she could feel around her. Ross swung the little girl up into his arms.

"Come on, Biddie-girl, sit with me. Look what Leia's made for supper. I'm starving, aren't you?"

"I don't wanna," Biddie whined, squirming.

Leia set several bowls down on the table and proceeded to serve the gumbo. "I've brought you a surprise, Biddie." The

137

child ceased struggling, and Ross hastily plopped her in a chair.

"What?" she demanded.

"Uh-uh." Leia pointed at the bowl. "Supper first. I'll bet a smart girl like you loves shrimp. You, too, Mom," she said, pushing another bowl in Pamela's direction.

"I'm not very hungry," Pamela said with a shake of her head.

"Me, neither!" Biddie piped.

Leia gave Pamela a now-look-what-you've-done look. "Then no surprise!"

"Maybe we'd better eat a little," Pamela told her daughter. "I want to see what she brought!"

"Okay." Biddie's acceptance was grudging, but she began slurping soup with a surprising appetite for one so small. Her mother smiled and picked up her own spoon.

"Hey, what about me?" Ross demanded. "I'm the one who's starving!"

"Changed your tune, have you?" Leia teased. She waved a full, steamy bowl under his nose. "What'll you give me for it?"

"Woman, you try me!" he growled, a mock-fierce expression on his face.

Leia set the bowl down in front of him. "Yes, but what'll you give me?"

Ross caught her arm and pulled her closer, whispering something in her ear that made Leia blush a delightful shade of rose. "Okay, ladybird?"

"Dream on, flyboy," she tossed back flippantly. She hastily applied herself to her own bowl of gumbo to hide her flaming face. Excitement and need quivered through her, but she forced the feelings down. It didn't matter that she wanted to rip Ross's clothes from his lean body and ravish him; Pamela needed their support right now.

138

"I'm through!" Biddie announced. "Can I have my surprise?"

Leia made a production of dramatically inspecting the child's bowl, noticing with satisfaction that she had eaten well and had lost her petulant, irritable look. Pamela had finished as well and gave a satisfied sigh. Leia smiled, then retrieved a bag from the cabinet and placed it in Biddie's waiting hands.

"Oh, a bear dressed like Santa Claus!" Biddie exclaimed, burying her pert nose in the soft velour fur and stroking its red velvet suit. "Thanks, Leia! Can I go show him to Bubba?"

"Sure, but can I go, too? I'd like to make Bubba's acquaintance again."

"Yeah!"

There was general laughter as Biddie hauled Leia down the hall toward her bedroom. Before long Leia was seated cross-legged on the floor, discussing Bubba's winter wardrobe and making up stories about Santa Bear. They got Bubba dressed for bed, and Leia gently encouraged Biddie to put her nightgown on as well. She could hear the soft clink of dishes from the kitchen and then Pamela's and Ross's voices in the living room practicing the cadences of the childbirth breathing techniques. After a while Biddie curled up in Leia's lap as she read some books out loud. The child clutched Bubba and her new bear, her head nodding.

" 'The end.' " Leia put the last book down. "Getting sleepy?" she asked.

"Uh-uh. Leia?" Biddie hesitated, then her voice was thin and hesitant on a question that had been clogged up inside her all evening. "Did—did you bring me the bear 'cause my daddy isn't coming home anymore?"

"Oh, honey, no! Of course not," Leia said, her heart twisting.

139

"But Mommy and Uncle Ross were talking and . . . and . . ." Biddie stammered to a halt.

"And it's all so confusing and frightening, isn't it?" Leia's voice was gentle. "Things have happened and your daddy might be involved, but they don't know for certain yet. My godmother always says it's best not to borrow trouble. Do you know what that means?"

"No." Biddie's voice was very small.

"It means you shouldn't worry about something until that something actually happens. I'm sure your mom will tell you as soon as she knows anything about your dad. She trusts you. She's counting on you to help her with the new baby. Big sisters are very important, too, you know."

"They are?" Biddie's words were laced with drowsiness.

"Yes. Anyway, the reason I brought you this bear is that when you're worried, sometimes it's good to have someone to hold on to. Someone you can tell your troubles to. So when you're feeling low you just hold on to this old bear real tight, okay?"

"Okay." Biddie cuddled deeper into Leia's lap. Leia hummed and rocked gently and soon heard the soft, repetitive rhythm of Biddie's breathing settle into slumber.

"Looks like both the Anderson gals have given it up." Ross stood at the door, looking down at Leia with Biddie in her arms, a warm light in his eyes. He could imagine Leia holding another child, *their* child. The vision was vivid with hopes and dreams that came from deep in his soul. "No, don't move. I'll get her."

He pulled back the covers of the twin bed, then lifted the sleeping girl and tucked her in. Leia got stiffly to her feet.

"Pamela's asleep, too?" she whispered.

"Yup. Those relaxation exercises worked like a charm." He snapped on Biddie's night light, turned off the overhead

140

fixture, and ushered Leia into the hall, closing the door behind them.

"Good. She certainly looked as though she needed the rest." Ross's wide shoulders filled the narrow hall. Leia took a step toward the kitchen, but Ross caught her about the waist and backed her up against the wall.

"I need something, but it's not rest," he said, nuzzling the curve of her neck.

"Oh, Ross," she said with a sigh. She slid her arms around him, smoothing her palms up and down the rolling muscles in his back.

"Do you think you could hold on to this old bear real tight?" he asked.

She gave a start of surprise, then smiled against his mouth as it found hers. "You were listening," she said accusingly when he raised his head.

"You're so good with kids. I know you'll be great with our kids, too. How many babies do you want?"

Leia's breathing stopped, then returned in a long shaky gust. Babies? Ross's babies. Why hadn't she considered that before? A little piece of Ross to hold in her arms, nurse at her breast, and call her own. Something melted deep in her heart. "I don't know how many."

"I've always wanted a houseful, but I'll consider stopping after five or six."

"Six!" she squeaked.

"Shh! You'll wake everyone up," he cautioned, grinning. "We'll discuss this further after we're married."

"Ross, you're rushing—" His mouth stopped her words, and suddenly she didn't care. The special magic of his lips and touch sent every thought but him right out of her head.

"I'm glad you're here. You're so good for me," he said at last. His voice was husky. Her head rested on his shoulder, and his large hand threaded through her red-gold curls.

141

"I know you're worried about Webb," she murmured quietly. "Is there anything you know that you're not telling Pamela?"

"No. We know his squadron scrambled to intercept hostile aircraft, and fire was exchanged. There are muddled reports. Some say no damage, some say several had to ditch. We just don't know."

"Oh." She shuddered and clung to him.

"What?"

"I just keep thinking, what if it were *you*? I couldn't be as strong as Pam."

"Yes, you could." He pulled back slightly and tilted her face so that he could see her in the hall's dim light. "Pam made her choices a long time ago. Webb and I both accepted the price that we might have to pay when we swore our oath of allegiance. And we've all chosen to live rather than to merely exist. You're a survivor. You will always do whatever you have to."

"You have such faith in me that it makes me ashamed," she murmured.

"I don't want you to feel that way. But courage isn't a lack of fear. It's getting a handle on the things that scare you and learning to deal with them. You control them. They don't control you. I know you have that kind of courage, Leia."

"I do when I'm with you. I'm working on it, Ross. I really am."

"That's all I can ask." He kissed the tip of her nose. "As much as I'd like to continue this talk in a more private place, I guess I'd better try to reach the duty office again."

"And I'd better be getting home. You will call me, won't you?"

"You know it. Just as soon as we hear."

But there was nothing new to hear all the following day.

142

And Leia wasn't even surprised when neither Ross nor Pamela showed up for the regular Tuesday-night childbirth class. Even the ten o'clock news had nothing substantial to offer, other than contradictory comments from every Washington official who would allow an interview. Leia finally went to bed, discouraged and frustrated.

Ross's call woke her just after midnight.

"Webb's okay."

"Ross! Are you sure? Really?"

"Yes, really!" His relieved laughter boomed over the receiver. "Pamela just spoke with him on the telephone. He engaged a hostile and took some damage. He was forced to ditch. It took them a while to find him, but he's okay. And there's been no further trouble."

"Thank God!" Silent tears of relief at the happy outcome of Webb Anderson's ordeal slid down her smiling face.

"God, I'm beat."

"Where are you?"

"At Pam's."

"Would—would you like to come over?" A rising heat colored her cheeks. It blazed crimson at the long silence.

"Where are *you*?" he asked, his voice raspy.

"In bed."

"Wearing?"

She smiled, tempted to say *nothing* but finally deciding the truth was temptation enough. "A long green silk gown slit up the sides with spaghetti straps at the shoulders. But . . ."

"But what?"

"If that doesn't suit, I could always change into something more . . . comfortable."

He groaned. "Damn! You know I'm awful partial to spaghetti in any form, but . . ."

"But what?" she parroted him.

"I'm really wiped out, ladybird, and the Blues fly to El Paso tomorrow. Next-to-the-last show of the season this weekend. Had you forgotten?"

"I suppose I had." She sighed her disappointment but then remembered what Pamela had said about worrying more when your man didn't put his flying first. "Maybe you'd just better go home. I want you back in one piece Sunday night."

"This is going to be the longest damn weekend on earth!" He groaned again.

She laughed softly. "Do we have a date for Sunday night, no matter what time you get in? I'll wear my spaghetti."

"That sounds—delicious. I'm already starving!"

"So what else is new?" she teased.

"Woman, you have no pity. Yes, we have a date. I love you."

"I love you, too, Ross. Hurry home, darling."

Leia hung up the phone and snuggled back down under her warm covers. Her last conscious thought was that it was indeed going to be the longest weekend on earth.

The longest weekend on earth passed, and by Sunday afternoon Leia was a bundle of nerves. She'd done her nails twice, cleaned the house from top to bottom, typed the minutes to the Seville Square Merchants Association Christmas planning meeting, and she still went into a semidaze every time she thought about Ross. Two of the biggest, thickest steaks in all of Pensacola waited in her refrigerator. Her table was set with her best lace mats. Her bed was made with a new set of designer sheets. She wondered if it would be too obvious if she met him at the door in her green silk gown. She wondered what her mother would think if she knew her only daughter was planning the seduction of a slow-talking Tennessee farm boy who flew jets for fun! She wondered if she could live with Ross. She wondered if she could live without him!

Leia looked at the clock and knew that if things kept going at this rate she would surely explode from tension long before Ross and his teammates flew back into town. She needed a run, she decided. That was it! A short jog to take the edge off, relax her a little. She pulled on her most ragged pair of gray sweat pants and a faded jersey the color of old pea soup. There would be plenty of time to shower and do her hair before Ross arrived. She jogged down the street, mulling over in her mind the dilemma of the green silk gown.

Gray clouds scudded overhead and the wind had an element of chill to it, but Leia was warm with exertion. She was delayed on her round, once at the Anderson house to check on a now vibrant Pamela and a once again irrepressible Biddie, then delayed a second time by a wide detour around a rather unfriendly dog of alarming proportions. It was an hour and a half later. Her breath was ragged, and she wiped her sweaty forehead with a grimy hand, then rubbed the dampness off on the sagging seat of her sweat pants. She turned the last corner onto Garden Street and slowed to a walk, puffing like a locomotive. She felt infinitely more relaxed, rather like a limp noodle.

Suddenly her complacency vanished in a puff of smoke and she jerked to a halt at her driveway entrance. There sat a fire-engine-red Corvette, and coming toward her with a high-voltage grin on his handsome face was none other than the object of her thoughts!

"Oh, no!" she wailed. "What are you doing here?"

Ross's face fell comically. "Don't we have a date?"

"Not yet!" she practically yelled, seeing her plans for a sophisticated seduction go up in flames. She scraped back her stringy, sweat-dampened mop of hair and glared at him. "Don't look at me! I'm a mess!"

"Is that all?" He laughed and reached for her, but she ducked under his arm. She bounded toward the porch, dug into her jersey for the house key on its frayed shoelace, and unlocked the door. Ross followed her, his warm laugh rich and sensuous. He caught her arm just inside the door and swung her around, pinning her up against his blue-uniformed chest. "Don't I even get a hello kiss?"

"No! I'm all sweaty and yucky and I stink!"

"So what?" he murmured. His lips covered hers, and Leia was lost. What the hell? she thought dizzily. If he didn't mind her sweating on his uniform, why should she?

"You're early," she said when he lifted his head.

"I take full credit for the fastest debrief in Blues history, ladybird. I missed you too much to be late."

"Well, you spoiled your surprise."

"I did?"

"There was going to be this seductive vision, all curled and perfumed and dressed in a slinky green gown, meeting you at the door. Too bad."

"Hmm. Should I go out and come in again?"

"Sorry. It was a once-in-a-lifetime opportunity. You'll just have to take what you can get now."

Ross chuckled and he kissed her forehead. "That'll do just fine, thank you, ma'am. Leia, don't you know that even salty and disheveled, you're still the most beautiful thing in the world to me?"

Leia's initial annoyance dissolved completely. What other man could ever make her feel this special? She smiled up at him. "Commander, you do have a way with words."

"That's not all I intend to have my way with," he said with a growl.

Leia laughed and shivered, but she tugged gently free of

his hands. "Promises, promises. Let me get a shower first. Are you hungry? I've got steaks ready in the fridge."

"Sounds good."

"Will you put them on?" she asked, moving toward the bath. "I'll be right back."

"Sure, go ahead. But don't take too long."

Leia grabbed a few things from the bedroom and ducked into the bath. She turned on the taps and ruefully pushed aside the assortment of bubble bath and body oils with which she'd intended to pamper herself. There wasn't time for that now. Stripping rapidly, she pulled up the nozzle, slid shut the shower curtain, and stepped under the spray. Grabbing her favorite strawberry shampoo, she worked up a lather in her hair, letting the hot water wash away the dirt and fatigue. Closing her eyes, she ducked under the nozzle to rinse.

The screech and rustle of the shower curtain startled Leia. She opened her eyes, gasping and spluttering under the spray. Ross, naked as the day he was born, calmly climbed into the tub and tugged the curtain back in place.

"What—what are you doing?" she asked inanely.

Ross's grin was wicked, his muscular body overpoweringly male inside the confines of the shower stall.

"Dinner will have to wait," he said, and reached for her.

CHAPTER NINE

"Wash my back, will you?"

Leia blinked, drops of water weighing heavily on her lashes. Mesmerized, she took the bar of soap Ross offered, her senses reeling. She finally had him right where she wanted him, and he wanted her to wash his back? He vigorously scrubbed his chest with soapy hands and then presented his back to her, but Leia saw the wicked twist of his lips. So he wanted to play games, did he?

She worked up a soapy lather, then began to rub his back, starting at his nape. The first instant of contact was like an electrical shock racing up her arms. She smoothed suds across his broad shoulders, down the valley of his spine, into the twin indentations at the top of his taut buttocks. She felt his jerk of surprise and began to enjoy herself.

"Let me get the rest of you," she murmured, sliding her hands under his arms around to his flat stomach. She pressed her front against his back and continued to wash, enjoying the texture of his hairy skin beneath her fingers.

Ross groaned, and every muscle in his body twitched. The points of her breasts felt like hot pokers on his back, and her hands were doing magical, delicious things, sliding, slipping against his skin in slick sudsy abandon. How he'd missed her! She was a constant revelation, ever the lady, yet fully a woman for him. The shower beat down on them like hot rain, drumming out a tempo against his skin that echoed the thunder in his bloodstream.

Ross began to feel light-headed. He braced his hands on the opposite wall, his head hanging between his arms, his ears ringing. Her fingers slid over the sensitive coin of nipple, dipped into the well of his navel to tantalize, then inched downward to the throbbing part of him. With a strangled cry he turned around, pulled her against him, and blindly sought her mouth. It had been a hundred years since he'd held her, and he knew his restraint was near the breaking point. One more touch and he'd surely go off like a rocket. Water streamed off their faces, coursed downward, parting where their bodies joined like a river flowing around a rock.

"My turn," he said hoarsely. He ran his soapy hands down her shoulders, across the sensitive underside of her arms, then slowly traced the outline of her ribs. Leia's lips were parted and trembling, her eyes half-closed with pleasure. His palms swept around the globes of her small, perfect breasts, the white suds partially hiding the rosy crests like flowers under the snow. Ross turned her slightly, watched in fascination as the water rinsed the suds away, revealing her again to his avid gaze. He bent, sipping the beads of water from each turgid nipple in turn, his hand moving down, parting her thighs, seeking entrance between the warm, moist petals that guarded her womanhood.

"Ross!" she moaned, leaning helplessly into him, her hands frantic on his broad shoulders. She murmured incoherently against his wet head and his tongue rasped against her nipple, heating her need to the boiling point. The time for games was over. She clung to him, tugged him upward to find his mouth, kissing him with an ardor that told him in more than words her need and love.

Ross's mouth slanted across hers, his tongue masterful,

demanding, sweeping into that cavern to taste her fully. He reached for the water faucets and turned off the shower without releasing her mouth. The shower curtain was swept aside, and he lifted her to stand streaming on the tile floor. He wrapped a towel around them both, but his intent was soon forgotten as hands avidly explored and tantalized, and the terry bath sheet dropped to the floor unnoticed. Ross picked her up and strode purposefully into the bedroom.

The air seemed cool on Leia's damp, overheated limbs as Ross laid her gently on the four-poster bed. She shivered uncontrollably on the quilts; then he covered her with his body. She welcomed his warmth and weight with a tiny sigh. He was home. He buried his fingers in the damp strands of her hair, holding her head in place while his lips plundered the hot, silky sweetness of her mouth and she answered him, giving everything, holding nothing back. Hands caressed, explored, begged. Damp skin moved against damp skin, each nerve sensitized, each cell attuned to the singing litany of desire.

Leia gasped when Ross rolled over, pulling her on top of him.

"Open for me, love," he said, his voice raspy, his large palms guiding her hips toward the heated shaft of his body. He probed, then plunged upward, driving deep into the slick pulsating heart of her. Leia gasped, the pleasure of being one with him so intense it was almost a pain, but it was pain that became quickly exquisite, uncontrollable sensations carrying her away on the wild, bucking ride toward heaven.

Stars exploded behind her eyes and she cried out, soft, incomprehensible whimpers of delight. Ross's mouth was hot on hers and he swallowed up the sounds from her throat, devouring her, mating mouths as well as the other parts of their bodies. Leia arched, her body contracting, and she rejoiced, gladly accepting the gift Ross bestowed as, groaning, he spilled himself into her in a perfect act of love.

Leia collapsed on his chest, dazed and sweat soaked, every molecule of her body staggered by the enormity of her release, by the emotions that filled her and overflowed. "Oh, love," she crooned softly. There were no other words.

After a while Ross shifted, settling her on her side, then straightened the tumbled covers and pulled a sheet over them to ward off the chill from their love-dampened bodies. He lay on his side, ear resting on one arm, the other hand cupped possessively around the curve of her hip. His eyes silently charted the purity of her features, the swollen outline of her lips, and his expression was filled with tenderness.

"Yes," he said softly, "love. Unbelievable that a rounder like me should find the perfect little ladybird like you. Do you know how special, how rare what we share is?"

Her smile was misty. "I think so. I'm not so very experienced, but nothing has ever moved me like you do."

"Well, I am fairly experienced—maybe more than you'd like—but I can tell you that nothing—no one—has ever moved me like this either. Do you understand why I can't imagine spending the rest of my life without you?"

"Oh, Ross." Her hand stroked his cheek. Her voice caught. "I can't imagine it either." She felt his instant tension, and his hand squeezed her hipbone in a reflexive reaction.

"Then marry me."

"I'm afraid."

His eyes narrowed and his jaw tightened. He pulled away, sitting up on the side of the bed, staring at the wall. "You can't have it both ways, Conner. I can't take it. You're using me."

"No!" she cried. She reached out, touched the bony arch of his bent back, but he jerked away, shooting to his feet.

He swayed, caught himself, ran a hand over his eyes in what seemed a gesture of defeat. She saw him swallow, then walk resolutely to his pile of neatly folded clothes on her dresser. A minute later he zipped himself into his flight suit. He studied her tousled reflection in the mirror, and his voice was flat.

"Next Sunday's performance is my last as a Blue Angel. A couple of days later is the end-of-season party. The day after that I close my apartment. I'm going, Leia, unless you can give me a reason to stay."

Panic fluttered in Leia's stomach. She got up, reaching for her robe. "Couldn't you stay for a while? I need time . . ."

"I want to see my folks. It's beautiful this time of year in Tennessee. I was hoping to make it part of our honeymoon trip. And I report to Miramar January second." He turned to face her. "I can't accept a long-distance relationship without knowing where I stand. If you don't want me, then send me away."

"Ross, please!" Raw pain glittered in her eyes. She hung on to a bedpost, hovering at the end of the bed in confusion.

"Dammit, Leia! What do you want from me?" He bore down on her, capturing her arms in his big hands. She stood miserably between his bare feet, her head bent, her voice trembling.

"Understanding. It's something I can't do lightly. And then there's the shop and Elizabeth to consider."

Her words angered him, and he shook her. "Dammit! What about us?"

"I'm trying!"

"It's not good enough!" he shouted. He drew a deep breath, battling for composure. "Just a simple gold band, Leia. That's all it takes."

"Don't you think it's what I want, too?" she cried.

"Is it? We keep going around and around and never getting anywhere! Why, Leia? Isn't our love worth it?"

"Love dies." The words were out before she was conscious of forming them. She raised her stricken blue-green eyes, and her breath caught on a sob.

Ross's jaw clenched, and his expression was grim. "I see. Stephen died. Mitch died. It's not fear of my flying that's keeping us apart. You're afraid of making the commitment. You owe your love and loyalty to dead men, and there's nothing left for me!"

"That's not true." But her voice was strangely uncertain.

He shook his head and laughed, a sad sound that echoed in the little house. "Never mind, ladybird. Stay in your safe little nest. I can't make you fly with me. And it hurts too much to try anymore."

His hands fell from her shoulders, leaving her stunned. She watched him scoop up his shoes and socks, then walked unsteadily out of the room. The crash of breaking glass broke the spell of immobility.

She rushed into the living room. Ross was down on one knee, gingerly picking up the broken pieces of a ceramic lamp from the hardwood floor.

"Sorry," he muttered.

"Leave it. I'll get the broom."

"No, I'll clean it up." He blinked, then shook his head as if to shake off a pesky fly.

"What's the matter?" Clumsiness was the last attribute in the world Leia would ever assign to Ross. And she didn't think he'd shoved the lamp off the table in a fit of anger. Her instincts said something wasn't right. She touched his arm. "What's the matter?" she repeated.

"Just a little dizzy, that's all. I haven't eaten, I guess."

"Then let me feed you. It would be a shame to let those steaks go to waste."

"I don't think so."

"Please, Ross." She took the shards from his hands and set them in a pile. "What difference will it make? Please stay. Just for a while."

He looked at her uncertainly, the golden flecks in his eyes glowing in turmoil. His gaze took in the thin silky robe, the aureole of damp red-gold curls that framed her face, the vulnerable curve of her lower lip. His glance fell to her dainty feet, and his throat worked. "You'll get cut. You're barefoot."

"You are too."

"So I am." He swallowed, trapped by the turquoise appeal in her eyes. "Steaks, huh?"

Her smile trembled and fought valiantly to stay in place. "You want yours rare?"

"The rarer the better. Just warm it through. I'm hungry enough to eat it cold."

She let out the breath she'd been holding. "Sure. Relax. I'll take care of everything."

They crept around the little house as if the entire structure had been built on quicksand. The broken lamp was quickly removed and the steaks broiled to crisp, succulent perfection and immediately consumed. Conversation was awkward. Leia watched Ross with an eagle eye for further signs of dizziness, relieved that a hearty meal seemed to be all that he needed. She invited him to stretch out on the sofa with the Sunday paper while she washed the dishes. To her surprise, he did. To her further surprise, he was sound asleep when she finished.

She padded about the house, tidying up, quietly checking on him from time to time. He slept a long time while the chilly November wind whipped through the night, cutting around the corners of the cozy house and whistling under the doorjambs.

Changed and showered, she curled up in the chair at his side and brushed her hair, watching him sleep, the feelings of love and loss tumbling headlong within her soul. Was what he'd said true? Was she afraid to commit herself completely to any man? Had the trauma of losing Mitch and the cool, egocentric nature of her father warped her ability to love completely? Or was it merely an excuse?

She studied the straight line of Ross's nose, the power in his jaw, now relaxed. She longed to run her fingertip across the bushy length of his eyebrow but dared not disturb him, sensing his exhaustion. There would never be another man like Ross, not for her. Yet when she thought of joining her life with his, a choking irrational fear clawed with icy talons at her heart.

She must marry Ross or lose him, and she didn't blame him for giving her an ultimatum. He'd been more than patient. Yet somewhere deep inside she was convinced that by marrying Ross she'd be signing his death warrant. She was a jinx, a black cloud, the angel of death all rolled into one. The flyers she loved died. She couldn't take that risk with Ross's life. She loved him too much. She shook her head, fearing herself slightly mad. It was easier to let Ross go than to burden him with her fears, a burden that might be the cause of his death. Hadn't Pamela told her that the wrong kind of wife could be deadly? And hadn't Leia herself tried to warn Ross from the very beginning that this ending was inevitable? A single, silent tear rolled down her cheek.

Ross stirred, stretching on the couch. He blinked, focusing on the sultry vision standing at his side. Leia stood silhouetted against the golden glow of the lamp, her soft curls a halo lit to incandescence, her slender form draped in emerald silk. Tiny straps held up a lacy, minuscule bodice, and the fabric caressed her creamy skin, accentuating the jut of her hipbones, the concave region of her navel, even the

155

small mound at the top of her thighs. Her face was shadowed, mysterious. Slumber fell away from him like daybreak.

"Leia?" He hardly recognized his own voice, so thick and husky. After all that had been said, he still wanted her. He would want her forever.

Gracefully she sank down beside him, never taking her eyes from his face. Slowly she pushed one thin strap down her shoulder, freeing an alabaster breast. She took his hand and filled his palm with her flesh.

"If I can't give you what you want, love," she whispered, "let me give you what I can."

There comes a point in a man's life when he has to accept the fact that his body can betray him, Ross thought. He watched the woman he loved sleeping at his side, her face pale and lovely in the early morning light. Her breathing was soft, barely lifting the sheet that covered her breasts. Her small hand rested beside her cheek, open and childishly vulnerable. She slept deeply, exhausted by a night of lovemaking that had been tinged with desperation on both their parts.

He knew in his soul that what she had offered him—all her sweetness, all her passion—was her way of saying goodbye. But just as desperately, he had sought with all his skill, all his love, to bind her to him in an intimacy so strong that good-bye would be impossible. Only her waking would tell the success or failure of his attempt. He could not face the reality of that just yet. So he watched her sleep.

Oh, God, ladybird. How can I live without you?

A terrible sadness grew within him, squeezing his chest, forcing the air from his lungs. Had Ross Walker, hotshot, finally met the defeat that would break him? He swallowed painfully and eased from her bed. A pool of emerald silk lay on the floor beside his wrinkled flight suit. He picked both up and crept silently from the room.

Zipped into the flight suit, he buried his face in the gown, inhaling the lingering fragrance of her sweet perfume. He took a deep breath and draped the gown over a chair, then a wave of dizziness overtook him. He walked unsteadily into her kitchen.

Coffee. That was what he needed. Something to chase the cobwebs out of his brain. His vision was fuzzy and his ears rang. He fumbled with the coffee filter. Suddenly the world tilted, shifting to an outrageous angle. The coffeepot clattered to the floor. Cursing, he hung on to the edge of the cabinet while the room spun crazily.

"Ross! Ross, what is it?"

Leia's gentle hands held him. He tried to answer by shaking his head, but that was a mistake. He was rolling out of control, and he clenched his jaw on a wave of nausea, unable to balance himself.

"Here, sit down," she urged.

Which way was down? Which way was up? Ross shut his eyes on the topsy-turvy world. Unable to find his own way in a universe suddenly gone directionless, he had to trust her. It was hard—his body was betraying him in a totally unexpected way. He lurched, holding on to her shoulders, felt the chair beneath his thighs and sat down—on the ceiling? He bent forward, his head between his knees, breathing hard, willing the vertigo to end.

"Here, an ice pack may help. It's the only thing I can think of," Leia said.

Ross gasped at the icy towel she draped around his neck, but the nausea receded. He rubbed his face with the towel and slowly sat back. Gingerly he opened one eye. The world was back in place. He opened the other eye, hardly daring to move his head. He licked his dry lips and blinked. Leia's lovely, worried face moved into his field of vision.

"Are you all right now?"

"Yeah." His breath puffed between lips stretched in a grimace and gradually returned to normal. "I'm okay."

"You're not okay! You're lucky you didn't fall flat on your face. Did you talk to Pete Neely about this?"

"About what? I just had a little dizzy spell. I had a lot of pressure in one ear yesterday that was bothering me. It must have cleared finally, that's all."

"Ross, be reasonable. You can't fly in this condition. It's not the first time it's happened. It's an inner ear disturbance, maybe even Ménière's disease like my father has——"

"It's not Ménière's! And I'm not your father!" he snapped angrily, sitting up. Fear and anger strummed discordantly across his nerves.

"You've got to face it. You've got a problem and it might be serious enough to ground you permanently."

"There's nothing to face! Give me some credit! I know if I'm all right or not!" His voice was hostile, defensive even to his own ears.

Leia's lips parted in disbelief, and her eyes widened as though she were seeing him for the first time. "You've never considered it, have you?"

"What?"

"The possibility that something could end your flying career. Things happen, Ross! You're not going to be young forever! Eyes go, or blood pressure. So it happens to be an inner ear thing for you. Didn't you ever think it could happen?"

He stood, pushing the chair back with a harsh scraping sound, and glared at her. "Oh, you'd love *that*, wouldn't you, Leia? That would solve all your problems! Well, it's not happening! I'll fly, come hell or high water, and you've got to make a choice—so don't pray for the easy out!"

Her expression was horrified. "You'd ignore something physically wrong, risk yourself and your teammates? I thought you had more integrity than that! I thought you were different, but you've got that same damn fighter jock ego as all the rest!"

Fury rose in him at her denunciation and he clenched his fists, refusing to defend himself. "Lady, you've got that right. I make no excuses for who I am."

"For God's sake, Ross! You don't have to fly an airplane to prove you're a man!"

"Maybe not, but you've got to be woman enough to let me do what I have to do."

Her face was pale and stricken. "All or nothing? Then I'm not the woman you want."

Ross stared at her, feeling his jaw work with tension. He looked away from the pain and fear reflected in her eyes. He forced out a breath and his words were flat, hopeless. "Then that's that, I guess."

He looked around for his shoes, remembered seeing them in the bedroom, and went after them. When he returned, Leia was on the phone, speaking softly. She turned as he approached, holding out the receiver to him.

"It's for you."

Puzzled, Ross frowned. He hadn't heard the phone ring, and he didn't want anything to delay his flight from the hurt, accusing look in Leia's anguished blue-green eyes. Reluctantly he took the phone.

"Hey, Hickory! What's all this about?" Pete Neely asked.

Ross's answers to the flight surgeon were monosyllabic, and his eyes drilled into Leia, pinning her motionless while his rage at her betrayal grew white hot. "I'll be there," he said at last to Pete, knowing his choices had been taken from him. Slowly he hung up the phone.

"I had to do it, Ross," Leia said. Her hands twisted in the silky fabric of her robe.

"I'd never fly if I weren't fit."

"I had to be sure." Her eyes filled with tears. "Please let Pete check you out."

"I don't disobey direct orders. I'm to meet him at the base hospital in an hour."

"Can I drive you?"

"No."

"You were acting so unreasonably," she said, begging for his understanding. "I was so afraid, so worried . . ."

Ross's expression was stony. "You don't have the right to worry about me, not anymore. Only a wife has that right."

"Oh." Her single word held a wealth of pain.

"I should have listened to you. I see now that your fears will always keep us apart. I guess deep down I always knew a lasting relationship was impossible. You built a wall I couldn't fly over, ladybird. Still, I had to try."

"Your ego can't let you admit that maybe some of my fears are valid." A tear slid down her cheek but she didn't wipe it away. "I can't live with someone who thinks he's Superman, Ross. But I had to try, too."

Hazel eyes met turquoise ones. The few feet that separated them might well have been measured in light-years.

Ross swallowed, hating the cold lump that swelled in his throat, cutting off the words he knew she wanted. He was thankful that there was no pain, only blessed numbness. He reached out and touched the glistening tear hanging from her lashes with his fingertip. It was warm. His hand dropped.

"I'll see you around, Leia."

"Sure." She forced a tremulous smile, knowing that he lied but there was nothing she could do to challenge the

160

reality of their failure together. "Promise me—" Her voice caught and she began again. "Promise me you'll be careful up there, okay?"

"Always, ladybird."

He bent to kiss her cheek, and Leia's eyes closed. His lips were warm, then all too swiftly he was gone. Leia did not open her eyes until the front door had slammed behind him.

"All right, gentlemen, that'll do it."

The Boss dismissed the Blues in his Oklahoma drawl. Chairs scraped back noisily from the table in the debriefing room of the squadron offices. Team members and trainees filed out, talking and joking. Ross remained sprawled in his chair, absently toying with the wire stems of his sunglasses, his thoughts preoccupied.

"Hey, Hickory! You comin' to the 'O' Club tonight?" Marc Garret asked. "The newbies are buyin'."

Ross glanced up, shrugged. The room was clearing rapidly. "I suppose, Miami." He couldn't work up any enthusiasm at the prospect. He knew he wouldn't be very good company, but then he didn't have anything better to do, did he?

"Come on, Hick! You got to celebrate! Last show of the season tomorrow. Got to go out with a bang, not a whimper!"

"I might drop by at that."

Hell, it was better than nothing, he thought, dropping the sunglasses into his pocket. He couldn't face another lonely night in his empty apartment. He didn't even think he could bring himself to give Pamela and Biddie a call. It had been awkward enough making excuses to back out of the last childbirth preparation class the past Tuesday night, but he just couldn't bring himself to go through that torture. Pam was no dummy. She'd picked up on his vibes immediately.

161

She knew that something was wrong, but she'd made no comment until after she'd been to class.

"You're not going to tell me, are you?" Pamela had asked him when he'd dropped in to check on her.

"There's nothing to tell."

"She looks just as miserable as you do. Oh!" Pamela gasped and placed her hand on her swollen stomach.

Ross was on his feet in an instant, helping her to sit down. His face was anxious. "Are you all right?"

Pamela laughed, rubbing the small of her back. "Of course. It's just a twinge. I've been having Braxton-Hicks contractions for several weeks now."

"Contractions!" Real alarm colored Ross's voice.

"Relax, Ross. If you'd been more conscientious in your class work, you'd know that it's perfectly normal."

"Oh." His smile was rather sheepish.

"And I said that Leia looks as miserable as you do." Pamela placed her hand on Ross's. "Is there something I can do? I'll be glad to talk to her if you think it will help."

Ross shook his head and looked away. "It's hopeless. But thanks anyway."

"Funny, that's what Leia said."

"She did?" Turmoil fluttered in Ross's stomach.

"Yes, she did. And I told her the same thing I'm going to tell you."

"What?"

"That for two people who are so right for each other, neither one of you can see the forest for the trees! And you both need a swift kick in the hindquarters!"

Reluctantly Ross laughed, a sound that was suspiciously thick. "I wish it were that simple."

He'd gone on to talk of other things then——Webb's return, whether Pamela would brave the crowds in her condition and bring Biddie to Sunday's farewell air show, how his packing was coming. But it was all just a cover, a way to try to hide from Pamela and himself that he felt as though his heart had been torn out of his body, and there wasn't a damn thing he could do about it.

It was a feeling that didn't go away, and he cursed himself for being a damn fool. He snapped shut his debriefing log and stuffed his pen into the narrow pocket on the right arm of his flight suit. Sitting here stewing about it wasn't going to do him any good. He just had to accept the fact that he'd lost his ladybird. There wasn't really any point in setting blame. It was just best that he didn't see Leia again. He closed his eyes on the hot blade of pain that sliced through his insides.

A large, friendly hand pounded his shoulder, and he heard the Boss's gravelly drawl. "What's the matter, son? You look like you just lost your last friend. You okay?"

"Sure, Boss." Ross cracked a smile. "Pete ran enough tests to drive me off the deep end, but I checked out. There's a little fluid left in that ear, but he gave me something powerful to dry it up. I'm fit."

"Hell, I knew that, son, or you wouldn't have flown today," the Boss said dryly. He hitched a hip onto the table and stared down hard at Ross. "It ain't your ear that's the problem, it's your mental attitude. Your flying's okay, but your concentration's shot. I want to know what the hell's the matter."

Ross straightened. "I'm sorry a personal matter interfered with my performance, sir. It won't happen again."

"Can the crap, Ross. This is man-to-man. Scuttlebutt says you and Leia have split."

Ross bit back an expletive. "Isn't anything sacred around this place?"

"Family is family." The Boss shrugged. "I'm sorry about

163

it. I could have sworn she was more than just another one of your babes."

"Yeah. Me, too." Ross sighed. "She tried to tell me from the first that she couldn't hack it. Then this thing with the ear broke the camel's back." He gave Chuck Lohman a long look. "She went to Pete first when I wouldn't," he confessed.

"You got a problem with that?" There was a hint of a challenge in the Boss's voice.

"Wouldn't you?" Ross was surprised.

"Hell, son. You might be a grand hand with the ladies, but you ain't had *any* experience with a wife. Melinda's had to pull me up short plenty of times when I was feelin' too big for my britches. We got our eyes on the sky, but a woman who loves you keeps her feet firmly planted on the ground. Kinda balances out, you might say."

"You make it sound easy."

"Uh-uh. Hard as hell. A constant battle to compromise. Ya see, son, a Navy wife may never know what it's like to do what we do—the speed, the hunt, the surge. On the other hand, we can never really understand how they feel, sending us off every morning, sayin' good-bye, knowing that, well, anything could happen. Takes a lot of courage on both parts. But you know what?"

"What?"

The Boss rubbed his jaw and gave Ross a wry look. "It's worth it. If that li'l gal isn't just another one of your good-time girls, you'd better think hard about lettin' her get away."

Ross's brain worked furiously. Had he been expecting too much from Leia? Taking it all, and never giving anything back? Could he accept her concern for him as genuine, as part of the process of loving and not something he could dismiss as an irrational outgrowth of her flying phobia?

Maybe he had to accept that her loving him gave her the right to care. And he knew they both still loved each other. Could he let her walk out of his life without making one more try?

"You know, Boss," Ross said slowly, giving his commanding officer a thoughtful glance, "you could be right."

The Boss grinned and clapped Ross on the back again. He slid off the table as Ross stood. "Come on, son, I'll buy you a cold one."

Ross glanced at his watch. He gave a slow grin, and his voice was filled with new determination. "No, thanks, sir. I've got something important to do."

CHAPTER TEN

Leia set the crown of orange blossoms on the bride doll'
golden curls and straightened the filmy tulle veil. The doll'
satin dress was lace appliquéd and encrusted with beadin
and pearls, truly a collector's choice or a little girl's dream
Her fingers strayed briefly across the bodice in admiration
It was such a lovely creation that even a grown-up gir
would love to wear such a dress.

For Ross, her mind whispered, and instantly tears pricke
behind her eyes. But then it didn't take much to set her o
these days, these centuries, since he'd left. No matter ho
hard she lectured herself, how many times she reminde
herself that she'd made a happy escape, she knew she wa
merely chasing a delusion. It was going to take a long tim
to get over that flyboy.

She swallowed back the lump in her throat and deter
minedly set about restocking the doll display. Despite th
fact that Thanksgiving was still a week away and althoug
the air show had taken place on the base today, there ha
still been many customers in The Gingerbread House seek
ing that perfect Christmas present. She would be glad t
close the shop shortly and get out of her shoes!

The little bell tinkled over the door, and Leia stifled
sigh. Another last-minute shopper. She heard steps behin

her. Forcing a smile to her lips, she turned and said the words she'd uttered at least a thousand times today.

"Can I help you . . . ?" A soft gasp escaped her. Ross. Tall and lean in that electric blue flight suit, his hazel eyes warm yet uncertain, he lacked for once at least a small iota of his usual self-confidence.

"Yes, ma'am, I sure hope you can," he said.

"What are you doing here, Ross?" Pain made her voice sharper than she'd intended. Didn't he know that seeing him was like pouring salt into an open wound?

"Well, actually, I was hoping you could help me with this." He offered her a paper scrawled with his bold handwriting.

Leia took the paper automatically, looked at it curiously, then with growing incredulity. "You—you're Christmas shopping?"

"Well, yes. For my nieces and nephews. See, here are their names and ages and sizes. Their moms make sure I'm informed. The doll I got here for Biddie was such a hit, I thought maybe dolls for the girls, sweaters or something for the boys."

"I see." No, she didn't see at all! Why was he doing this? Surely he wasn't so insensitive? She forced down the quivering inside her and squared her shoulders. Business was business, right? After all, it was all she had, right? It was surprising how little comfort one found cuddled up next to a cash register. She forced herself to be crisp, businesslike. "Did you want dolls like Biddie's? We still have several anatomically correct—"

"No, ah," he spluttered, a rosy wash glowing under his tan. "Just plain dolls will be fine. The folks back in Tennessee are a mite old-fashioned about such things."

"No problem." What was she saying? This was a gigantic problem! She could hardly be civil to the clod! How could he discuss presents when all she wanted to do was throw her arms around him or at the very least kick him in the shin for putting her in such a situation? She saw Elizabeth' frowsy gray bun bobbing behind a rack of dresses and tried an easy way out. "Elizabeth? Could you come help a customer please?" Leia didn't realize how desperate she sounded.

"Why, hello, Commander." Elizabeth's sharp eyes peered at each of them with avid interest.

"Miss Elizabeth," he acknowledged. But he was not going to allow his plans to be ruined. "I hope you don't mind if Leia helps me with these selections. I feel they need her undivided attention."

"Not at all, dear. Call if you need me." Chuckling to herself, Elizabeth went back to her work.

Leia groaned inwardly. "Very well, Ross. Let's see what we can do."

Leia went around the shop in a veritable flurry. Teddy bears for the youngest nephews, dolls for the girls, sweaters and suspenders for the older boys, gloves and fancy stockings for the preteen girls. She wrote out the ticket, added it up laboriously, then recklessly, for no good reason, discounted the entire bill by a large percentage.

He signed his charge card slip with a flourish, not even glancing at the total. So much for that gesture, she told herself. "Will that be all?"

"Could you wrap them? Separately?" His voice was all innocence.

"Of course." She ground her teeth to keep from screaming. Or bursting into tears. She located boxes and began wrapping each gift in bright red and green Christmas paper. She was supremely conscious of Ross lounging beside the counter, watching her every move. Deftly she made the firs bow and taped it to its box. She was cutting the trailing ends of the ribbon into precise angles when he spoke.

"I like to watch your hands, ladybird. I think I began to fall in love with you when you were wrapping Biddie's birthday present."

Leia jumped and the scissors slipped, digging into her finger. "Ouch! Damn!" The scissors clattered to the floor and Leia sucked the cut.

"Here, let me see." Ross was beside her, tugging her hands into his grasp.

"It's nothing." Leia's voice was ragged, his touch unnerving her.

"You're bleeding."

"I'm okay."

He held her hands firmly, then slowly lowered his mouth to the tiny cut and kissed it. Leia shuddered. "Ross, please."

"What's the matter?" Elizabeth asked, bustling over.

"A little accident," Ross replied. "Could I get you to finish wrapping these things, Elizabeth? I'll take Leia out for a breath of air."

"No! I'm all right!" Leia was frantic, but Ross urged her toward the front door.

"You go ahead. This won't take but a few minutes," Elizabeth promised. "And turn over the Closed sign as you go out, will you?"

Ross complied, then all but carried Leia across the porch and down the steps of The Gingerbread House. He marched her across the narrow street toward the open parklike area of Seville Square. It was almost dusk, and a few children played on the swings at one end. The heavy branches of giant oak trees rustled with the wind off the bay, and the chill cut through Leia's silky dress.

"Ross, please!" Leia cried. "What do you want?"

"I have to talk to you." His tone was hoarse. She felt so

slight under his arm, so perfect. He hustled her out of the wind into the large open gazebo that graced the center of the square.

"Please, oh, please," she said, her voice choked, suddenly near tears. "Don't you know how badly this hurts?"

"Believe me, I know."

Her eyes were wide and luminous with pain. "Then why?"

He gently pushed a tousled red-gold curl back from her face and swallowed. "I can't give up on us, ladybird. I know I was an ass the other day, and I'm sorry. I was wrong to try to shut you out."

"You—you saw Pete?"

"Yeah." His smile was wry. "Needles and tests and being poked and prodded. I'm fine. It's definitely not Ménière's. He cleared me, and I flew today."

"I'm glad, Ross. I—I didn't want that for you."

"I know. I guess it happened for the best, though. I learned something very important—that Superman needs Lois Lane to watch out for him. Give us another chance, Leia. I promise I won't forget again."

Leia's fingers pressed against her trembling lips. "Why do you have to be so damn perfect?"

"What?"

Her laugh was a hollow sound that echoed against the gazebo rafters. "It's not fair, you know. Most men have at least one flaw. The other day I thought I'd discovered yours. I grabbed onto it like a drowning man. When you wouldn't admit you were sick, I thought, There it is! There's the real reason I can't marry Ross. It was an excuse, something that made me feel slightly less neurotic. I could blame you instead of myself."

"What are you saying?"

"I'm saying that you've shown me growth and maturity,

and a willingness to compromise—and sent everything I feel back to square one. You don't play fair, Ross."

He smiled. "Not if it gets in the way of what I want." He caught her shoulders and pulled her close.

"You don't understand. You've changed, but I haven't. Now nothing but your career stands in our way, just as it has from the very beginning."

"So?"

"So I can't bear to start over, just to have it end the same way. It hurts both of us too badly."

He frowned. "I don't like the sound of this."

She backed out of his grasp, her eyes wide with pain, her voice choked, "I'm sorry, Ross. I'm sorry I can't change. I'd only make you unhappy in the end."

"Only if we're apart. Let me help you change," he began.

She turned away, leaning against the railing, and tried to control the wobble in her voice. "It's no use. Something like that has to come from inside and I just don't have it. It's better this way. Only a fool keeps hoping when there is no hope."

He was silent as he studied the shape of her slender back, the shoulders turned away from him. A muscle worked in his jaw, then he walked purposefully toward her. Placing his hands on her shoulders, he bent and tenderly kissed her temple. His murmur was low in her ear. "Then count me a fool, ladybird."

He left her, striding away toward the shop, reappearing moments later with his arms laden with colorful packages. Leia watched him drive away in absolute despair, certain that she was doing the only kind, the only merciful thing for both of them. With leaden feet she walked back to The Gingerbread House.

"You're letting him go, are you?" Elizabeth asked when

171

her goddaughter came through the door. Her hands were fist-down on her chunky hips in a belligerent stance.

Leia clamped her teeth on her bottom lip to still its uncontrollable trembling. She got her jacket and purse from under the counter and began digging for her keys to lock up. "I couldn't do anything else," she muttered. "Besides, I have responsibilities to you and the shop."

"That's the most godawful foolishness I ever heard!" Elizabeth said with a snort. "We can always work something out. I'll buy you out, or we'll hire help and you can hold on to your interest. But none of that is important! That man loves you. Are you blind or just a fool?"

Her words struck a nerve. "What do you want me to say, Elizabeth?" Leia demanded. "I'm not the woman he needs. I don't want to hurt him with my fears. I'm not going to risk marrying him, only to end up like my parents! That would be worse than not having him at all!"

"Ross Walker is nothing like your father. Can't you see that? Your father would never have come to your mother like Ross just did for you. Maybe if he had even once, their marriage might have held together, even after Stephen died. If he'd shown Elise that he would try to meet her halfway, they could have made it work."

"It doesn't matter," Leia replied, despondency blowing through her soul like an arid wind. "I can't be the kind of brave, risk-taking wife Ross needs and deserves."

"Can't?" Elizabeth said scoffingly, frowning in disapproval. "Or won't? There's a difference."

Leia tried to swallow a sudden lump of self-doubt; then her heart faltered at Elizabeth's final scathing words.

"Maybe you're more like your father than you think."

Elizabeth's words echoed in Leia's brain, stalked through her dreams that night, and woke her to the morning's sunshine with no bright promise of the future, only an aching

172

emptiness. Losing Mitch and Stephen had hurt, but it was nothing like the meaningless void that filled her now.

She puttered around the Sunday emptiness of her house, shades of Ross in every nook, every corner, haunted by the memory of his touch, his loving. The knowledge that he would be flying his final performance as a Blue Angel in a matter of hours beat on her brain. Then he would be gone for good, out of her life forever. Suddenly it was imperative that she see Ross again, if only from a distance.

Leia threw on jeans and a windbreaker, then drove through the thick Sunday afternoon traffic to the naval air station. She felt a compelling need to say good-bye in her own way, to prove to herself she had enough courage to bring their brief, flaming affair to a dignified end, at least in her own mind. There could be no unfinished business taunting her through the years with what might have been. Ross was a Blue Angel, one of the Navy's finest aviators. The least she could do was accord him the respect due that position by watching his final performance, even though to do so would be sheer torture. But it was the only way to prove to herself with total finality that she was doing the right thing, not only for herself but for him as well.

It was a case of déjà vu. At Sherman Field she wandered along the airstrip among the displays of aircraft, past the souvenir stands laden with shirts and hats and inflatable plastic jets, moving through the bustling throngs of happy air show spectators. But this time she stayed away from the cordoned-off VIP stands, finding a place instead beside the crowd barrier well down from the center of the flight line. She had an unrestricted view of the six blue-and-gold Hornets gleaming in the sun, waiting to be fired into action.

Her heart thumped in her chest and her mouth was dry, but she forced herself to watch everything. The ground crew worked industriously, their efficiency evident in every move they made around the aircraft. An officer used specialized equipment to test wind conditions. Military pride was displayed in every aspect of flight preparation here at the Blue Angels' home field. It was remarkable, even awe inspiring.

A dark car rolled out to the center of the field, halted, and six men in electric-blue flight suits climbed out. Leia watched the distant figures approach the grandstand, walk along the barrier shaking hands and signing autographs on proffered programs. She mentally went over the roster: the Boss, Skip, Alcatraz, Sandy, Miami, and Hickory.

The routine began, and everything was the same. The introductions, the tight line of planes taxiing down the runway, the thundering roar and flash of heat and speed as the Hornets took off. Tension built inside Leia. The wind whipped her hair about her face and she pulled the tendrils back, staring up into the clear, sunny sky. The diamond formation reappeared, and her hands clenched on the metal railing of the crowd barrier.

What was Ross feeling? she wondered. What was he thinking during this final show as a Blue Angel? Was he sad? Or did he rejoice in the pull and thrust of his aircraft, winging his way over the crowd? Or perhaps he wasn't thinking at all, instead merging with the plane into the complex fighting machine that was one of the Navy's finest weapons. In another month he'd be training to fly another kind of aircraft, getting ready for a tour of duty out of the limelight but showing the same dedication and fierce pride in himself and his country as he did today. It was a way of life as necessary to him as breathing. Today wasn't really the end for him, merely the start of a new beginning.

The narrator's voice boomed over the loudspeakers, announcing the maneuvers performed by the diamond and the solo pilots: echelon roll, tuck-under break, fortus, double farvel. Leia's fingers tightened on the barrier and her eyes followed the speeding jets in their aerial ballet. The crowd ohhed and ahhed at each fantastic maneuver, applauding their approval after each successfully executed stunt, but she was silent and watchful, licking dry lips.

The diamond loop. Her heart faltered at the announcement, the remembered terror of Ross's New Orleans crisis shivering down her nerves in cold waves. Yet, fascinated, she couldn't turn away. This was Ross at his best, doing the work he loved. What right had she to fear for him? None, for she'd sent him out of her life. Yet she couldn't deny the invisible cords tying them together, for now and for all time. No matter how far he went away from her, he carried a thread from the skein of her existence, and that thread was love.

The jets tore down the flight line toward her, then, noses lifting, the tightly fitted diamond rose like a kite in a freshening breeze, up and up into the sunlit sky, floating upside down for that breathtaking, interminable moment, then skidding down the inside of the circular loop, noses pointing toward the earth.

Images flashed like lightning across Leia's mind. The here-and-now faded as the four diamond Hornets screamed toward the ground. Stephen's bomber going down in the jungle. Mitch's spiral nose dive to the depths of a California forest. Four blue-and-gold jets plummeting into the tarmac. Blinding explosions, flaming debris . . .

Leia gasped. Cheers drowned out the thundering beat of her heart. Intact, the Blue Angel diamond rounded the bottom of the loop, shrieking past her as easily as a child pulls the ribbon on a package. No death-filled fantasy this, but reality as welcome as the first rose of April.

Leia swallowed and swayed, her knees weak. She had to make an effort to unclench her fists from around the metal bar she held. Raising trembling fingers to her lips, she stared after the retreating diamond. It took another effort to examine the nerve-shattering vision her subconscious had thrown at her.

Ross dying in a crash. She'd seen it. It was the worst thing that could ever happen to her. *The worst thing.* And yet . . .

She looked deep into her soul and knew for a certainty that if it ever happened, somehow she would survive. She was strong. The possibility of losing Ross to a fate of his own making was a destiny she could accept. That wasn't the worst thing. The *worst* thing was losing him without ever knowing the joy of sharing her life with the man she loved. She'd missed that chance once with Mitch. She could never survive that kind of loss again. And here she was *choosing* that same fate! The inner light of self-revelation was a small flame in her mind that grew and grew to a beautiful, blinding brightness.

Ross had told her once she was afraid to live. He'd been right. What she hadn't been able to accept then was that living itself was a risk. In her determination not to let herself be hurt ever again, she'd constructed a wall to keep the world out, never knowing what she had been missing until Ross flew over that wall with all his tenderness and gallantry and humor. Suddenly everything was clear and simple. What she stood to gain in choosing to love Ross far outweighed what she would undoubtedly lose if she never took the chance. Despite all her fears and misgivings, it was as simple as that. And she knew that she had to take the chance.

A warm feeling of hope swelled within her breast. She smiled, suddenly aware of the easing of a long-standing ache deep within her soul. It was as though Stephen and Mitch stood beside her, their love and understanding reaching out to her across the barriers of time and space. At last she could say good-bye, let them go. There would always be a place in her heart for them, yet an inner peace filled her, and she knew that she had their blessing.

The feeling of closeness faded just as the six-member delta formation flashed overhead, crossing and recrossing in a vertical break that left the crowd gasping and cheering. A soaring joy filled Leia and she laughed out loud, no longer viewing the spiraling jets as an avenue of sure death but rather as a celebration of life. Eagerly she watched the delta swoop down to earth, settling gently with a simultaneous screech of tires, flashing past her toward the end of the runway. She found the gold number three of the left wing plane and followed Ross's progress back to the reviewing stand.

She struggled through the press of the crowd, eager to see him, to touch him, to *tell* him. But no. She stopped, biting her lip. She couldn't tell him of her change of heart and mind so abruptly, in front of thousands of strangers. It was something reserved just for the two of them. A nagging doubt erupted. What if he didn't understand? What if he didn't believe her? She had been adamant enough just hours before. Would he doubt her sincerity?

Leia drew a deep, sobering breath, her ears echoing with number seven's roll call of Blue Angels. She straightened her shoulders, and her chin lifted. Somehow she would convince Ross that her love was strong and her new resolve unshakable. She'd take a page from his own book and overwhelm him with confidence. A tiny nervous shiver raced up her spine, but she ignored it.

There was nothing to do but take the chance, but not here, not now. She'd choose her time—later after the final debriefing, after the inevitable let-down of a final performance. As the crowd applauded and cheered Leia turned away, secure in her determination. Her lips curved upward in a soft smile as she headed for the souvenir stand. Maybe the place to start was right here.

177

                              * * *

Leia knocked softly on Ross's door, then plunged her
trembling hands deep into the pockets of her windbreaker.
The glow of the street lamp cast her shadow in stark relief
against the condo's cedar siding, and the wind whipped
sharply across the waters of the bay. She turned, staring
hard at the sleek lines of Ross's red Corvette parked in the
drive. Surely he was home? Light glowed from within the
apartment, but she didn't hear anything. Screwing up her
courage, she knocked again.

The door opened and Ross stood there, a Ross unlike any
Leia had ever seen. He wore a pair of old cords, faded and
worn to softness, and a white short-sleeved undershirt that
clung to his chest like a lover's hand. His brow was puckered
in an irritated frown, but it faded to wary inquiry when he
saw her.

"Hi." Leia's voice held a breathless, throaty quality she
could not control.

"Leia." He swallowed. Good lord, he thought, what is she
doing here? She looked about sixteen, her face surrounded
by those tumbled red-gold curls, her hands jammed defensively into the pockets of a disreputable old windbreaker.
Her jeans outlined the slim beauty of her shapely legs, and it
was all he could do not to reach for her. He resisted the
impulse, the solemn uncertainty of her features quelling his
sudden surge of hope.

"Can I come in?" she asked hesitantly.

He backed off, tugged his ear, and shrugged. "Sure. I
guess."

She followed him into the apartment, noticing the litter of
half-filled boxes, open cabinets, and empty bookshelves. He
shoved a cardboard box off the breakfast table and set it on
the floor.

                              178

"Sorry about the mess," he muttered. "I've been packing."

"So I see." She could have groaned at the inanity of her words. Licking her dry lips, she wondered how to begin. Where was all her glib self-confidence now? She wandered over to an open box, lifted out a shiny loving cup and studied the inscription. A football trophy from Cumberland High School to one Ross E. Walker. Odd to think of Ross that young.

Ross cleared his throat. "Was there something you wanted, Leia?"

The loving cup slid back into the box with a soft crash. The look she turned on him was confused, hopeful, scared. You, she thought wildly. I want you. She glanced away from the warm hazel depths of his eyes, nervously zipping and unzipping the front of her jacket.

"I—I wanted to tell you . . ." She swallowed and began again. "I saw you fly today."

He crossed his arms and frowned, struggling with his surprise. "You came to watch the show?"

"Yes." She nodded, her voice a whisper, her eyes wide blue-green pools.

Ross's heart thumped madly in his chest. This was totally unexpected. Leia had purposefully placed herself in a situation she would find unbearable? "Why?"

"At first I wanted to say good-bye," Leia said. She saw his face fall, felt his dismay, and tried to hurry on. "Then it—"

The strident ring of the phone cut across her words. Ross leapt to answer it, reaching for it like a drowning man, glad for anything to stay the hated words coming from her awhile longer.

"Hello? Who? Biddie, slow down, honey," he said into the receiver. "I can't understand . . . What! I'm on my way."

He slammed the phone back into its cradle and reached for a leather jacket.

"What is it?" Leia asked, alarmed at his sudden agitation.

"The baby's coming!"

"Whose? Pam's? But it's too early!" Leia cried.

"I know." His face was grim. "But Biddie said that Pam said to come quick. I've got to get over there."

"I'm coming with you!" Leia said, her tone adamant.

Ross gave her a quick, hard look, then nodded. "Come on, let's go."

They hurried outside, heading for Ross's car. Leia stopped long enough to grab her purse from her car and, as an afterthought, the medical kit she always carried. The ride to Pamela's was a blur, and for once Leia didn't mind Ross's speed or his skill with the wheel.

Ross didn't bother to knock at Pamela's. He burst through the door, only to come up short, finding Biddie seated on the couch beside Pamela, holding her mother's hand while a look of intense concentration scored Pamela's face.

"I'm helping Mommy with her breathing," Biddie announced proudly.

"That didn't take long," Pamela said as she panted, trying to smile. She struggled to stand. "I think we'd better hurry."

"Wait a minute, Pam. How far apart are your pains?" Leia asked.

"I don't know. Two minutes or so, maybe less."

"Why didn't you call before now?" Ross demanded.

"They didn't get bad until just a little while ago. My water broke," Pam said. She smiled. "Don't fret, Ross. I won't make you come into the delivery room." Another contraction gripped her and she sank back down, breathing through her mouth in the rhythmic Lamaze method.

Leia ran her hands over Pamela's distended abdomen, feeling for the position of the baby, checking the strength of the contractions. She turned to Biddie with a bright smile. "Biddie, can you do something very important for me?"

"Yes, ma'am." Biddie nodded, her piquant face serious.

"I want you to go next door to the neighbors and tell them what's happening. Ask them to please call an ambulance for your mom, okay?"

"Okay. I'll go tell Mrs. Shelton." Biddie hopped off the couch. "Be right back!" she said brightly.

"Ross, help me get Pam to the bedroom so I can examine her," Leia said.

"Wait a minute, don't you think—"

"Move it, Commander! Unless you think Pam would rather have this baby right here!"

Ross complied, lifting Pamela and carrying her back to her bedroom without further comment. Leia rushed ahead, grabbing a clean sheet from the hall linen closet and spreading it under the laboring woman. She pushed Pam's damp, tangled hair back from her face.

"I'm going to have a look at you, okay, Pam? Ross, you check on Biddie and see she stays next door, then haul your tail back here. I'm going to need you."

A minute later Leia pulled the sheet modestly over Pam's upraised knees and knew she had been right about needing Ross. She grinned and spoke cheerfully. "Looks like you're going to have this baby in the comfort of your own home, Pamela."

"Is it going to be all right?" Pamela asked between pants for breath.

"Sure. Everything looks just fine, except this little fellow is in a big hurry! Don't you worry!"

Ross rushed back into the room. "How is she doing? Could we take her in the car?"

"Uh-uh. Not enough time. Come on, coach," Leia said. "We've got work to do."

Leia saw Ross swallow harshly, glancing hurriedly at Pamela. Leia could have laughed at the changing expressions that chased across his face: anxiety, reluctance, acceptance, determination. He sat down at the head of the bed and began to arrange pillows.

"Come on, Pam!" he said. "Cleansing breath, focal point. We practiced all this, although as I recall, this was supposed to be Webb's part!"

"Sorry," Pamela said with a groan.

"Keep it going, but don't let her push yet," Leia instructed, peeling out of her windbreaker down to her new T-shirt. "I've got to scrub." She headed for the bathroom, failing to notice the strange look Ross gave her. She returned with her medical kit and some blankets she found folded in the nursery.

"I want to push," Pamela said between clenched teeth. Quickly Leia checked her again.

"Go ahead, Pam, the baby's head is crowning!" Leia said excitedly. "Help her, Ross! Lift her back like we did in class."

They worked furiously, encouraging Pamela, Ross pushing her forward with each contraction, helping her to bear down. Pamela groaned, her face clenched with effort, holding tightly to Ross's hands.

"Here it comes!" Leia cried. "Oh, it's a pretty one! Come on, Pam, push! A head full of hair, too. Now the shoulders!" With a final push the baby was delivered. "It's a boy!"

Pamela's cries of delight and relief mingled with the strong wails of her newborn son. Using a bulb syringe, Leia rapidly sucked any mucus from the baby's airways, then wrapped him in a blanket and laid him on his mother's stomach. She couldn't help her wide grin of pride and looked up to find Ross watching her, a matching grin on his face. She knew they'd shared something neither would ever forget. The distant wail of a siren announced the approaching ambulance.

Leia laughed. "Now they come!" She busied herself with caring for Pamela while Ross dutifully admired the baby, checking his fingers and toes for his weary but proud mother. In short order the ambulance team appeared, skillfully taking things in hand, and transported mother and son to the hospital for observation. Ross rode with Pamela in the ambulance, while Leia stayed behind to clean up and then went next door to reassure Biddie that all was well and that she did indeed have a new baby brother for her very own!

"I knew it," Biddie said smugly.

After arranging for Biddie to stay the night with the Sheltons, Leia carefully drove Ross's car to the hospital. Pamela was resting comfortably, and Baby Boy Anderson, cleaned up and in his hospital blue blanket, was snug in his bassinet behind the nursery window.

"Admiring your handiwork?" Ross asked, appearing suddenly beside Leia in the nursery corridor.

"Not mine," Leia said softly, smiling. She hugged herself, her hands dug deep in her windbreaker's pockets. There was wonder in her voice. "A real miracle created out of love." She turned to Ross, saw the tired lines in his face. "Quite a day, huh? Does Webb know yet?"

"I notified the squadron duty office to get word to him. Another week and he'd have been here himself. Pamela's mother is on her way, too."

"You did a wonderful job."

He chuckled softly. "I think I'd rather go into a tailspin than do that again! And you were pretty handy yourself. Do you suppose Pamela's doctor will split the fee?"

"Not likely!" She laughed. Ross gazed down at her intently and she met his eyes, suddenly sobering. Slowly he reached out, and she froze. With the tip of his index finger he gently folded back first one side of her jacket, then the other. His eyes darkened to burnt gold. When he spoke his words were low and deliberate, as if he held himself in stringent control.

"Would you care to tell me what this means?" he asked, staring at the message emblazoned on her dark blue shirt.

Leia looked down, blushing. She'd almost forgotten. But the legend was plain for the world to see. Bold letters said FLY NAVY. The recruiting slogan had seemed self-explanatory this afternoon. But maybe he needed her to spell it out for him.

"Can't you read, flyboy?" she asked softly. Her fingers traced the white letters across the navy blue background. "It says I love you."

A jolt of pure hope shot through Ross. His fingers tightened on her slim shoulders, and his throat clogged. "What else does it say?" he asked huskily.

"It says I can't live without you, and if it's not too late, could you please want me again?"

"Too late?" He pulled her close, inhaling her sweet fragrance, feeling the softness of her beneath his hands. "Aw, ladybird, it's never been too late for us."

Her breath left her on a long, shuddering sigh and she pressed her cheek against his chest. "I thought it was, but when I watched you up there today, it came to me. There's nothing more important to me than loving you." She looked across the hall through the nursery window at the sleeping infants, and suddenly her eyes misted. "And nothing more important than someday holding your baby in my arms."

"Is this what you were trying to tell me tonight at my place?" he asked.

She nodded, and her voice caught. "Yes, but I didn't know how to start."

"That's simple, Leia. Like this."

He lowered his mouth to hers and the rapture was there again, consuming them, sealing them as one for all time. The shiny hospital corridor faded away and they found that plane where perfect communication is possible. She was trembling when he lifted his head. He kissed her eyelids, banishing the glimmering moisture, tasting the salt of her remorse, the quenching flood of her resolve. She touched his lips with her fingers.

"Oh, Ross. There's so much to say. When I saw you flying today, I knew you were right all along. Life is a risk, but without you, I might as well be dead. Only when I'm with you am I truly alive."

A pulsating happiness gripped Ross's heart. "Does this mean you're going to marry me?"

"If you'll have me."

His cheek creased with a grin, and although his words were teasing, his voice was shaky with emotion. "I'm glad to see that you've come to your senses. I guess I wore you down with my rugged good looks and boyish charm."

She laughed softly. "Among other things. I was smitten from the word go, flyboy. I'm just glad you didn't give up on us."

"I'm a very determined man." His expression was suddenly serious. "I know we can make it together, Leia."

"I know it, too—now. I suppose I'll always be a little afraid when you fly, but now I can put it into perspective. I accept it because it's part of you. And without you, I'm nothing."

"A little fear can be a good thing. It can keep you from making silly, fatal mistakes. And darlin', I'll bet my last wooden nickel that we both die of old age, in our beds, after making love!"

"What a lovely thought," she said, smiling.

"And I can't think of a thing I'd rather do than give you my baby." Ross's voice was tender-rough, thick with love.

Leia quivered, feeling she'd never fully deserve this wonderful man's devotion but vowing with all her heart to try. "I love you, Ross."

"I love you, too, ladybird. How fast can you plan a wedding?"

Leia grinned. "I think I might hit mach two or better, given the right incentive."

A fire blazed behind Ross's eyes and he pulled her close. "I think I can give you plenty of that," he said with a growl.

"I'll just bet you can," she said with a laugh, breathless. "But not here!"

He glanced down the corridor, saw the curious looks they were getting from the duty nurses, and grinned wryly. He tucked her hand through his arm and turned her down the corridor. "Maybe you're right. Let's get out of here. But first let's tell Pam."

They walked side by side down the hall. Leia clung to Ross's arm as though he might disappear, but her voice held a dreamy quality.

"Ross?"

"What, ladybird?"

"Do you think Webb Anderson will be *my* Lamaze coach?"

"What? Hell, no! That's my job!"

"I wouldn't have thought you'd volunteer to do *that* again!" Leia laughed.

"Forget what I said before." He stopped and swung her into the circle of his arms. "I intend to share all of my life with you."

"What if you're on sea duty, like Webb was?"

He frowned. "Don't even think it!"

Leia smiled and touched his cheek lovingly. "At least you'll be there for the important part."

Ross laughed and hugged her hard. His voice was husky. "You'd better believe it, ladybird. For the rest of your life."

Push
westward
toward
California's fabled
land and fiery lovers

Sands of Gold

Day Taylor

Discover how two families, the Morrisons and McKays, struggle to survive the turbulent settling of America's West in the mid-19th century. Follow as the fever for gold rages, as lawlessness and lust run rampant, and as two families are swept into a tempest which threatens their fortunes, their loves, their very lives.

☐ **Sands of Gold** 17585-2-16 $3.95
☐ **The Magnificent Dream** . . 15424-3-23 3.95
☐ **The Black Swan** 10611-7-43 4.50
☐ **Moss Rose** 15969-5-16 4.50

 At your local bookstore or use this handy coupon for ordering:

Dell DELL READERS SERVICE—DEPT. A1587A
6 REGENT ST., LIVINGSTON, N.J. 07039

Please send me the above title(s) I am enclosing $ _____ (please add 75¢ per copy to cover postage and handling) Send check or money order—no cash or CODs Please allow 3-4 weeks for shipment

Ms./Mrs./Mr _____

Address _____

City/State _____ Zip _____